Navajo Sunrise

Ethan Flagg

A Black Horse Western

ROBERT HALE · LONDON

Typeset by
Derek Doyle & Associates, Shaw Heath
Printed and bound in Great Britain by
CPI Antony Rowe, Chippenham and Eastbourne

Navajo Sunrise

For the last three years Bearclaw Bat Madison has been searching for his wife, after her abduction by Indians from their isolated cabin near Snowflake, Arizona. Bat keeps his ears to the ground for any mention of a captured white woman.

His latest attempt to find his wife takes him into the Navajo homelands, but he soon discovers it is not his wife who is the captive. And this lady has a substantial reward on her head, offered by her fiancé for her safe return. Running into an old buddy from the past spells trouble and when the guy realizes who Bat is escorting, sparks begin to fly. . . .

ONE

TRADE OFF!

The dust-caked rider drew his mount to a halt.

Behind him stood a fully laden burro. The animal was reluctantly toting a host of trade goods.

The man removed his water bottle from where it hung on the saddle horn and shook it. The bottle was less than half full. From here on, every drop would need to be carefully rationed.

Cracked lips gingerly sipped the precious fluid. Although tepid and somewhat brackish, it tasted like nectar.

He untied a red bandanna and drew it across a sweat-beaded brow. His narrowed gaze shielded out the harsh glare of the sun. The golden orb appeared to issue a wry smile as it beat down with relentless fury, sucking the moisture from every pore of his body. A spring would need to be found before nightfall; more for the animals than himself.

Bearclaw Bat Madison had left Globe the previous week. Heading north across the Mogollon Plateau, he was now on the edge of Navajo territory. From here on he could expect that his every move would be under close scrutiny.

Since the disastrous resettlement of the tribe on the Pecos River at Bosque Redondo back in 1863, the Navajo had been resentful of any white eyes trespassing on to their domain. Known as the Long March, the forced removal of the tribe had caused severe hardship. The government plan proved to be a complete failure and eventually the tribe was allowed to return to its homeland in the northern canyons of Arizona.

Madison knew that, as a result, from here on he would need to proceed with extreme caution. Rumours had been circulating for some time that the Navajo were getting restive. The more irascible chieftains were pressing for revenge against the white invaders. They had started painting up, urging the more reluctant leaders to stiffen their resolve.

A final reckoning to square the shameful treatment that their forebears had endured at Bosque Redondo was long overdue.

Shongopovi was the name being bandied about as the chief most likely to instigate trouble. So far there had been little evidence of an uprising. A few skirmishes by recalcitrant young bucks, but nothing serious.

Yet!

The hairs on the back of Madison's neck prickled.

He shook off the unwholesome speculation that he was riding into a hornet's nest. Nervously, he nudged the paint mare forward. A barren, sandy wasteland stretched away into the distance. Soaring pinnacles of bare sandstone reached upwards to the blue firmament, sculpted into fantastic shapes by the wind.

Madison idly reflected how the Indians could manage to grow crops of pumpkin and beans in this unforgiving land. Life must be tough. Herds of sheep and goats were their main source of food. Yet survive they did, preferring life here to the squalid existence of the Redondo.

For two days he moved ever deeper into the tribal land with no signs of those he sought. Then, on the third day, he saw his first sign of life. A twist of smoke gently rose above the scalloped rim of the Chuska Mountains, the intermittent puffs clearly a signal to others that he had been spotted. It came as no surprise, judging by the massed ranks of sheep he was encountering.

The trader fingered the circlet of polished bear claws slung around his neck. So far any of the luck expected from the bizarre necklace had been mixed. Sure, it had kept him alive in dangerous situations. But his main reason for heading out into these wild places had thus far met with no success.

Numerous tales had been told around campfires as to how the enigmatic hunter had come by the bone appendages. Some said he had acquired them from an Apache medicine man who had cured an illness. Another rumour was that he had shot the grizzly that had killed his partner.

The most common theory. however, was that Madison had killed their owner in hand-to-hand combat. He had fought the animal with a knife after being attacked while camping in the Tonto forest north of Phoenix. When questioned, the hunter merely responded with a wry smile, relishing the aura of mystique the fabled necklace encouraged.

But Bat Madison had not knowingly placed himself in this currently dangerous situation merely to trade goods with the resentful Navajo. The news he had picked up in Globe was that a white woman was being held by the tribe in its northern enclave at Canyon de Chelly.

Every time he received such information, Madison made it his business to seek out the woman and buy her back from the tribe. He had been doing the same thing for the last three years.

That was the time his wife had been abducted from the isolated homestead he had built some five miles outside the town of Snowflake where he was town marshal. He blamed himself for the loss. He now realized that he should have accepted the mayor's offer of accommodation within the safety of the town limits.

Since that fateful day every report about the sighting of a white captive had sent him off into the wilderness. On each occasion he prayed that this time it concerned his beloved wife.

So far success had eluded him.

But he would keep trying, even if it took the rest of

his life. Maybe on this occasion the bearclaw charm would do the business and it would be his lucky day.

Madison's ruminations were abruptly interrupted by a feathered war lance burying itself in the ground immediately ahead. The paint whinnied in fright, rearing up on her hind legs. The trader forced himself to remain calm. The slightest hint of retaliation could find the next spear buried in his back.

Three braves appeared as if from nowhere in his path. Each held a bow and arrow pointed at the interloper's chest. Another two Indians cut off any escape to the rear. No words were uttered.

Carefully and with deliberation, Madison pointed to his laden mule and signalled that he was here to trade.

The leader of the group nodded, then swung his mount around and escorted the rider back to their camp. A cluster of hogans occupied a clearing in the canyon. Towering cliffs of orange sandstone rose up on either side. A shallow creek provided enough water to irrigate a few crops of beans and wheat sprouting from the parched land.

From the largest and most impressive of the octagonal structures emerged an equally grand Indian. He was clearly the chief.

A heavily beaded overshirt complemented the headband into which was sewn an array of eagle feathers. Each one depicted some heroic deed. Clutched across the broad chest was a war lance, also trailing feathers. The Indian was tall and statuesque, not unlike the craggy monuments surrounding the camp. Displaying a deceptively languid eye, the impressive figure watched the newcomer with a cynical mistrust.

Madison's own eyes widened. It was Shongopovi. His picture had been splashed across the front page of the *Globe Courier* along with the lurid headline: *Navajo Chief Set for Rebellion.*

The trader reined in his alarm, hands were raised in greeting.

Then Madison methodically proceeded to unpack the mule, laying out his wares on a blanket. All the goods were items that the Indians could only acquire from the white man: mirrors, needles, salt. The bolts of red yarn used in the weaving of blankets were especially valued by the womenfolk. For the braves there were tools and old flintlock rifles.

Once the items were on show Madison stood back, extending an arm inviting all to examine the goods. Their curiosity piqued, the Indians moved forward, rummaging about, open-eyed with childlike wonder. The mirrors in particular excited comments of glee from both men and women.

Madison stepped back scanning the huddle of hogans around the camp, avidly searching for a clue to the woman's presence.

'What you want for these?' the old chief demanded in a deep voice that resonated around the camp, instantly stilling the chattering babble. He was only one of a handful of Navajo who had learned the white man's tongue while struggling to survive at Bosque Redondo. 'We do not have the yellow rock that the white man always wants.'

'I do not seek gold,' replied Madison, accentuating his words with brisk sign language so that all the others could understand. 'Bearclaw Madison has heard that the Navajo people are holding a white woman. It is for her that I come to trade.'

Shongopovi's granite features remained inscrutable. A prickly atmosphere rippled around the silent gathering. Then he slowly raised his right arm. From the entrance to his hogan two squaws emerged, dragging a dishevelled-looking female. Her clothes were in tatters, her blonde hair was matted and dirty. The woman's head was lowered, leaving her face hidden.

Bat Madison held his breath, praying.

Nobody moved. All eyes were focused on the woman. Slowly she raised her head to reveal a drawn face smeared with dirt: her watery eyes were red-rimmed from crying. The trader sighed deeply. His shoulders slumped in disappointment. It was not Serena. But he did not allow his anguish to show.

He merely nodded. 'You keep all this in exchange for woman,' he said.

Shongopovi looked from one to the other. Then he picked up an old Springfield muzzle-loader, its barrel pitted with rust. His lip curled in disdain. Growling like a wounded grizzly, he threw it on the ground in anger.

'This no good!' A finger pointed towards the Winchester jutting from its scabbard on the trader's horse. 'Show me that!'

11

Madison shook his head. 'Not for sale.'

'Woman for rifle and goods, or you not leave here alive.'

It was a stark threat that saw the encircling braves moving in a step closer. Their weapons were raised awaiting the chief's signal.

Madison knew he was teetering on a knife-edge.

One false move and he was done for. Cautiously he moved across to his horse and extracted the latest '73 carbine. It had only been fired the once behind the gunsmith's store to zero in the sights. He was loath to part with the rifle, but had been given little choice in the matter.

'Show how to work,' ordered Shongapovi, grabbing the rifle and caressing its shiny stock. His black eyes displayed an avaricious gleam. Possessing such a weapon would make him invincible. A mighty leader above all the other tribal chieftains.

The next few minutes were spent instructing the chief in the task of loading and firing the prized repeater. Once completed, Madison moved away. With a measured prudence, he sidled over to where the woman had been left. The whole of the tribe's attention was now focused on the new rifle, the squaws included. It was time to leave.

But that was as far as he got.

TWO

A DEADLY CHALLENGE

A sudden sharp cry bounced off the enclosing sheer walls of the canyon. A tall young buck stepped forward. He was flanked on either side by two determined-looking bodyguards. They were not here to smoke the pipe of peace. Daubs of red and yellow pigment on their cheeks spoke of baleful intentions.

'No exchange woman for anything!'

Tocahatchi was the chief's son. He had been away hunting and had only just returned. With measured annoyance he threw down the carcass of a deer.

'Father promise woman to me,' he rapped loud enough for all to hear. 'Now I challenge white eyes for her. It is the law.'

All eyes turned to the newcomers. A tense murmuring replaced the excited babble of moments before. The trade goods were forgotten. This was a far more interesting development.

Shongopovi held up a hand, silencing the chatter.

His features hardened as he considered the challenge. Slowly, his patrician head dipped in a single nod of accord. 'Son is right,' he declared. 'You must fight him for hand of woman. So say Navajo law.'

Bat was caught between a rock and a hard place. There was no option now but to go through with the deadly duel. Refuse and he could leave. That was not a serious consideration. It would lead to him being forever shamed, treated as a pariah. And the woman would still remain here.

News of such things had a tendency to spread quickly through the Indian nations. No longer would he be treated with respect by other tribes in his continuing search for his kidnapped wife.

'I agree,' came the stoic response to the challenge, although inside his guts were churning faster than a runaway steam loco. 'But I choose weapons.' The chief nodded his assent.

The onlookers formed a wide circle with the two combatants in the centre.

Madison drew a large Bowie knife from the sheath attached to his shell-belt. He tossed it into the air, then caught the blade with his right hand and immediately threw it down to strike, point first, into the sandy ground.

Settling the matter by combat could take many forms. This one involved only a single knife.

Both men stripped down to reveal bare torsos. It

was up to the chief to signal the start of the contest. Shongopovi ensured that both combatants were positioned an equal distance from the knife. Stepping back he raised an arm.

Tocahatchi hunkered down, legs bent ready to lunge for the weapon. His opponent flexed tense muscles and fixed a flinty gaze on to the leering red face. A silence, thick as treacle, settled over the circular combat zone as both men waited.

The chief's arm dropped.

As one, they lunged for the knife. The Indian waited for his opponent to bend low, then chopped down with his right hand. The sudden blow was intended for the back of the neck. Instead, and luckily for Madison, it caught him on the shoulder. No damage was caused. But the ruse nonetheless worked in Tocahatchi's favour.

He grabbed the knife's bone hilt and dodged away ready for his next move.

Madison backed off out of range. The two men began gingerly circling each other, waiting for an opening. Both were fully aware that the Indian now had the advantage.

Tocahatchi smiled. His yellow teeth were bared in a savage rictus of arrogance as he began making short lunges with the knife. Nothing as yet to inflict any damage: merely brief feints to unsettle his adversary. Madison likewise was looking for an opening.

The nerve-shredding episode continued for five minutes. Another short jab came from Tocahatchi. But this time he followed through with a scything upward cut intended to rip Madison's chest open. The white man had expected such a manoeuvre and was ready. As he turned aside the slashing blade hissed by, no more than a whisker from his naked body.

He instantly grabbed the wrist holding the knife. The contest was now being fought in deadly earnest. Both men grappled for possession of the gleaming blade. Madison hooked a leg round that of the Indian, dragging him forward, off balance. The sweating pair of interlinked bodies tumbled to the ground.

The white man knew that he had to retain a firm grip of the Indian's knife hand. Let go and he was finished.

Over and over they rolled, slicked torsos coated in a layer of sand. Tocahatchi tried desperately to pummel his opponent's face with his free hand. The blows connected but they lacked any power.

Madison twisted the knife arm back, forcing the Indian to release the weapon. Still maintaining a firm hold of the same arm he fell on to his back, dragging the Indian with him but with his foot raised and pushed into the brave's stomach. With a single backward flick he tipped the man over his head.

Tocahatchi flew across the compound, crashing into the surrounding onlookers who scattered in confusion. Completely taken by surprise at this unexpected ploy, the Indian was left shaken. The numbing effect of the trick had befuddled his brain.

As he stumbled to his feet Tocohatchi once again

found himself dumped on the hard ground. Madison had slipped behind him, out of his field of vision. But on this occasion the sharp point of the knife was jammed into the brave's neck.

As he gripped the Indian's long black hair a growl of suppressed tension rumbled in Madison's throat. His eyes blazed with fury as his arm tensed, ready to plunge the blade into the soft skin and bring the contest to its bloody finale. A sigh of keen expectation rippled through the gathered throng.

Tocahatchi's eyes bulged. But they held no fear, no plea for mercy. That was when Madison realized the truth. To survive the death-dealing contest, having been bested by a superior opponent was bad enough. But to be beaten by a detested white eyes was shameful and degrading to an Indian. He would sooner die. But his life had been spared.

Now it was the white man's turn to smile.

Slowly he stood up and threw the knife down hard into the sand. The blade nicked the Indian's ear, then quivered in the static air.

For a full minute he stood over the defeated Indian, sucking great gulps of air into his straining lungs. The Indian stared back, his eyes bursting with hate knowing that he would become an outcast, condemned to wander the desert alone.

The victor was now free to go. Silently he deliberately turned his back, donning his shirt and hat. After fastening the gunbelt around his waist he kept a hand on the butt of the revolver while casually moving across to join the woman.

'Follow me,' he whispered, 'and don't make any sudden moves. That critter' – he nodded towards Shongopovi, who was still holding the Winchester to his chest – 'is likely to shoot us both down just for the sheer hell of it.'

The woman looked at him with dead eyes, her mouth agape, unable fully to comprehend what was happening. The notion that her nightmare incarceration might at last be at an end had not yet registered.

Bat helped her on to the burro. He mounted the paint and led the animal back down the trail, away from the Indian camp.

None of the Indians had moved. No words had been uttered as they silently watched the white man and his prize depart.

Another hour passed before either Madison or the woman spoke.

The tension was palable. Nerve ends jangled. Any second, Bat expected the ear-shattering roar of the Winchester to lift him out of the saddle. Only when the sun had dropped behind the western rim of the Chuskas was he able to breathe freely once again.

He led the burro and its rider into a narrow draw and made camp for the night.

The woman's name was Eleanor Newbold. She exhibited a muted disappointment on learning that her saviour was not an emissary sent by her fiancé. Howard Thompson was a wealthy landowner in Albuquerque who had made his money importing

American goods and selling them on to the Mexican traders.

'It was while passing through Globe that I heard about a white woman being held by the Navajo,' Bat replied in answer to her query.

'And you came all that way to rescue me?' The appreciative cadence in her remark brought a flush to Bat's tanned cheeks. He was more than grateful for the coating of dark stubble swathing his features and concealing his discomfiture.

'Seemed like the right thing to do,' he mumbled, shrugging off any thanks. He hadn't the heart to tell her of his regret on finding that she was not his missing wife. Meanwhile he busied himself cooking a simple meal of chilli beans and tortillas while a pot of coffee bubbled merrily close by. 'Vittles will be ready in fifteen minutes,' he added glad to change the subject.

Much to his relief the woman moved away to tidy herself up, using her rescuer's soap, flannel and towel. Upon her return to the camp, Madison failed to hide the shock betrayed by his bulging peepers and gaping mouth.

Eleanor Newbold was no plain Jayne, that was for darned sure.

Removal of the grime from her face revealed a smooth complexion that enhanced the endearing freckles around the pert nose. The freshly washed flowing locks of straw-coloured hair tied back with a red bow added to the dramatic transformation.

'Something wrong, Mr Madison?' she asked,

completely unaware of the effect her dramatic metamorphosis was having on the hard-boiled frontiersman. 'You look like you've seen a ghost.'

She didn't know how close to the truth the comment was. For the briefest flicker, the oval face of his kidnapped wife had swum into view. Just as quickly it had disappeared. But the vision had jerked Bearclaw Madison out of his stunned reverie.

Quickly turning towards the campfire, he grunted that the food was ready. Head lowered, he ladled the beans out on to a tin plate.

They ate the simple meal in silence.

After clearing away, Madison lit up a cigar and poured out mugs of steaming coffee which he perked up with a tot of whiskey.

He carried the liquor for personal consumption only, certainly not for trading. He had seen what hard liquor did to the red man. He wasn't used to it and didn't know his limits. The inevitable results were comical at first. But they often quickly degenerated into serious arguments where blood was invariably spilled.

Mellowed by the hot food and relief at now being safe, Eleanor told him how she had come to be taken by Shongopovi. She had been the only survivor of a small wagon train that was returning to Albuquerque from Farmington in the north-west corner of New Mexico territory.

'I had been visiting my sister who runs a saddle and tack store with her husband in the San Juan Valley. A large mule train leaves Farmington at the beginning of every month. But it was not due to depart for another week.' Eleanor paused to sip her coffee. 'So I decided, unwisely as it turned out, to accompany a group of settlers heading that way.'

She swallowed as a lump formed in her throat. Tears welled in her eyes at the recollection of her ordeal.

Bat waited patiently for her to continue.

'They attacked the wagons two days south of the Nageezi trading post. Heaven knows why they let me live.'

One of Bat's thick eyebrows lifted. He knew the answer to *that* all right. Eleanor Newbold was a handsome female. A prestigious catch for any young buck.

His own thoughts drifted back to the recent trial by combat. Although an unwritten Navajo law stated that the winner of such a contest should go free with no repercussions, Bat held serious doubts that it would be adhered to. He felt sure that Shongopovi would seek redress for his only son's loss of face.

They were still over a week's hard ride from Albuquerque. Plenty of time in this wild country for the Indians to mount a counteraction. And now the chief had possession of a new Winchester rifle, whereas he, Bat, would have to make do with a single-action Colt Frontier. A fine reliable weapon but no challenge to a fifteen-shot repeater.

Their safest option was to head for the trading post at Bitter Creek. It was solidly built to withstand onslaught from marauding Indians. More important, however, as far as Bat Madison was concerned, was the fact that it acted as a relay station for the Butterfield Stage Company.

With both parties musing on the same issue but from two completely different perspectives, the conversation lapsed into a pensive silence.

Bat threw the dregs of his coffee aside and tossed a couple of branches on to the dying embers of the fire.

'Better get some sleep, Miss Newbold,' he advised, handing over his bedroll. 'We'll need to be away from here at the crack of dawn to reach the trading post before dark tomorrow.'

'What about you?' asked the woman. Concern for her saviour's comfort was etched across her opalescent features.

Bat shrugged off her concern for him. 'I'll make do with the horse blanket. A mite smelly but warm enough.'

An owl hooted in the distance. Bat prayed that the haunting lament did not emanate from a more sinister origin.

He was up at the crack of dawn shaking the stiffness from cramped muscles. It had been a less than pleasant night. Every sound from the myriad of nocturnal creatures that called the desert home found him tensed up and edgy. The woman appeared to have spent an untroubled night secure in the illusory notion that she was now safe.

The mounts were saddled and watered before he saw fit to rouse her.

He wanted to reach the Bitter Creek trading post

by noon if possible, which would entail a hard ride across the broken canyonlands of the Chaco Sink. Once there, at least they would be relatively safe. Then he could ensure that Eleanor Newbold caught the weekly stage back to her fiancé in Albuquerque.

The guy would doubtless be frantic with worry.

They reached the relay station at two o'clock in the afternoon, thankful that there had been no signs of any Indians. The manager informed them that the weekly stage was not due until noon of the following day.

'Your wife can bunk in with Maisie if'n she's a mind,' proposed the manager indicating his own spouse who was clearing away the midday meal. 'You and me can sleep in the barn.'

Bat's face assumed a rosy hue. It was left to Eleanor to apprise the manager of their real status.

'Sorry about that,' apologized Chet Kingman. 'Just assumed the obvious seeing as you were travelling together.'

Bat hurried on to inform the guy of their current circumstances. Mrs Kingman invited the newcomers into the station for some freshly brewed coffee and a slice of her home-made pumpkin pie smothered in buttercream. She was a jovial woman of indeterminate age, well rounded in all aspects of her anatomy. In contrast, her angular pasty-faced husband was somewhat formally dressed in a black suit and tie.

In between mouthfuls of the delicious repast – a distinct change from the trail grub he had been used to – Bat explained how the two fugitives had come together. He intentionally omitted his own reasons for becoming involved in such a precarious enterprise.

Kingman was understandably concerned. Anxiety lines mingled with more permanent furrows that were age-related. 'Let's just hope they don't come after you. In my experience Shongopovi has always been a just and fair-minded chief where matters of Navajo law are concerned.'

'We can only place our faith in the good Lord,' added Maisie Kingman, casting a pious look towards the large crucifix on the wall. 'Another slice of pie, Mr Madison?'

THREE

PIKE ROSWELL

At about the same time as the events just related were taking place, three men had set up camp on the banks of a creek some five miles east of the canyon recently vacated by Bearclaw Madison and his female companion.

Pike Roswell and his two sidekicks had ridden all day since holding up the overland stagecoach just outside Winslow. They were bushed, plumb tuckered out. And not merely on account of the long ride. Things had not gone according to plan earlier in the day. As a result they were all but broke.

A tall, stocky dude, Pike boasted a thick moustache worn in the droopy Mexican style. His broad-brimmed Texas sombrero was pushed to the back of his head. As leader of the gang, he was a good fifteen years older than his two young associates.

Frank and Tom Craddock were brothers. Tom, the

younger of the pair preferred to be called the Coyote Kid. Roswell had picked them up in Tucson after they saved him from being gunned down by a back-shooter.

Mad Dog McFee had been trailing Roswell for the last two months claiming the outlaw had killed his brother. It didn't matter a hoot that Amos McFee had been caught cheating at cards. Fraternal loyalty demanded retribution, an eye for an eye as the Good Book dictated.

The two Craddock boys could have sympathized with that assertion. But shooting a man in the back was the action of a yellow-livered coward. According to their code of honour, the settling of such disputes could only be carried out man to man.

The Dog had been drinking all day in the Blue Diamond saloon when Pike Roswell sauntered through the door. The festering hardcase was barely able to contain his anger. But he knew about Roswell's reputation as a fast gun and had no intention of putting it to the test. Consequently he waited until Roswell left, an hour later, then he followed him outside.

Bleary-eyed and swaying, McFee drew his six-gun and aimed at the retreating back of his victim. At the same moment the Craddock boys emerged from the Apple Pie bakery, which was situated immediately opposite the saloon. They instantly took in the grim scenario about to be enacted on the far side of the street.

Without uttering a word, both men drew their

shooters and fired.

Orange tongues of flame and hot lead spat forth. Three times each pistol despatched its deadly load. The backshooter stood no chance. Dancing about like a cavorting marionette, his body slammed back against the wall. A dark smear of red was left behind as he slid to the ground.

Mad Dog's time on this earth had finally run out.

On hearing the lethal barrage, Pike Roswell reacted with the instinct that had kept him alive for so long. He dropped to the ground like a stone, gun palmed and pointing at the potential threat. Observing that the thundercloud threatening his continued enjoyment of life had passed over, he slowly climbed back on to his feet.

His two saviours crossed the street, their own weapons cocked and ready to finish the job if necessary. But the Dog lay unmoving on the sidewalk, his riddled corpse staining the woodwork a deep crimson. Dusting himself down, Pike wiped the sweat from his brow. He breathed deep, having realized just how close he had come to shaking hands with the grim reaper.

'Much obliged, boys,' he said, exhibiting genuine gratitude. 'You saved my bacon for darned sure.'

'We don't cotton to bushwhackers, mister,' Coyote told him, his elder brother concurring with a serious nod. 'Don't matter none to us what the reason was for your dispute. It should be settled face to face.'

Frank Craddock twirled his revolver on the middle finger of his left hand. Exhibiting a deft flourish, he flipped it into the air before catching the gun with the other hand and slipping it back into the oiled holster tied low on his right hip.

The trick had been performed without thought. The man was not trying to show off. But the action indicated to Roswell that these guys knew their way around hardware.

The men were clearly brothers. They had the same blond hair and lazy blue eyes which casually accepted the potential victim's thanks.

Pike took in their stance and the way they carried their guns, well kept and tied down low for ease of drawing.

The younger one had the look of a simpleton, but his curled lip appeared to challenge anybody who might choose to make fun of him. In contrast, his elder brother displayed a much more laid-back demeanour: an easy-going composure that could easily be taken for weakness. A fatal mistake, as Pike Roswell knew after witnessing the savage gunplay so recently performed. The young man's apparently relaxed manner could prove to be a veritable asset when the need for such action was demanded.

Pike was impressed. The two men complemented one another perfectly.

'You boys looking for work?' he asked in a casual tone of voice.

Coyote cast a questioning frown towards his older kin.

'Depends what you have in mind, mister,' Frank replied, warily stroking his stubbled chin. 'We ain't in the business of punching cows if'n that's what you have in mind.' Tom Craddock gave the remark a brittle laugh of derision. 'We kinda figure there's much easier ways to make a living.'

'You sure are right there, Frank,' Tom agreed, slapping his brother playfully on the back.

'Then it seems like you are just the sort of fellas I'm after hiring,' said Roswell with a smile. 'How's about we step back inside the Blue Diamond and discuss things over a friendly drink.'

Another look passed between the two brothers.

'What d'you say, brother?' asked Frank.

'Waaaal!' enunciated young Tom in his best West Texan drawl. 'We sure are getting low on funds. Can't hurt none to hear the man out.'

Frank offered an easy smile. 'Then lead on, Mister. . . ?'

'Pike Roswell's the handle.' The outlaw held out a hand.

'I'm Frank Craddock,' came back the brisk reply as the handshake was returned. 'And this is my brother, Tom.' A leery grin creased Frank's handsome looks. 'The Kid likes to be known as Coyote.'

Pike heard the nickname with a quizzical frown.

Frank explained. 'It's due to him having the bad habit of howling at the moon when he's had a skinful.'

Tom thought for a moment before the dime dropped. Then he slapped his thigh in protest at the tongue-in-cheek explanation.

'Don't you go believing this critter, Mr Roswell,' he

barked good-naturedly. 'It's just that I kinda envy their freedom to roam at will, letting other varmints do all the hard work.'

Ribald guffaws followed as the three men stamped back into the saloon.

That was how the new Roswell Gang came into being.

But any gunplay in an important town like Tucson was sure to attract the attention of the law.

Within ten minutes of the shooting the new gang had been joined at the bar by the local tin star. After questioning the trio, together with a couple of bystanders who had witnessed the fracas, he duly pronounced that it was a question of justifiable homicide. No further action would, therefore, be taken. Defending a stranger from being shot in the back was a thing to be heartily commended.

As a result the Craddock brothers earned themselves a free drink from the starpacker.

Pike Roswell, however, was less than pleased by the attention he was receiving from Marshal Ebenezer Gillfoyle.

'Have we met before, mister?' Gillfoyle screwed up his eyes in thought. 'Seems like your face is a mite familiar. Abilene maybe?' A brisk shake of the head from Roswell. 'Or perhaps Witchita? I was town marshal in that berg back in '68.'

'Never been anywere near either of them places, Marshal,' averred the outlaw, speaking with a firm assurance that was intended to settle the matter. 'You've got me mixed up with some other jasper.'

In truth, he had indeed crossed swords with the lawdog in the Kansas town of Witchita in that year. At that time it had been a hellsapoppin' end-of-track cattle town. Roswell had just spent six months on a Kansas chain gang for busting up a saloon in Abilene and he was ready for some action.

It was lucky for Pike that he now presented a somewhat altered appearance, which was why the marshal was struggling to place him.

In those days Pike had been clean-shaven and wore his hair much longer, in the style of his hero Wild Bill Hickok. After getting cleaned out at poker in the Saddleback saloon, Pike had robbed the general store of its week's takings. To compound the felony, he had then stolen a horse to escape.

That was the last time Gillfoyle had set eyes on the critter, until now.

Pike pulled his hat down low to keep his features in the shade.

Even so, Eb Gillfoyle still insisted on giving the outlaw some strange looks. Lawmen had the unwelcome knack of recalling all manner of faces. It went with the job.

Pike was sure that the marshal would be perusing his old Wanted dodgers back in his office. And Pike Roswell's description and current offences might well come to light.

He did not intend to be still around when the penny dropped. The sooner he was out of here the better. Pike and his two sidekicks hurriedly left Tucson soon after the local lawdog, having finished his questions, had left the saloon.

The Flagstaff stage was an hour late.

Coyote was getting restless. Pike was also concerned. He kept looking at his watch and shaking his head.

'Can't figure out why it's late,' he said for the third time in fifteen minutes. 'The Butterfield Company always prides itself on punctuality.'

Only Frank Craddock remained calm and unperturbed. 'It'll be along,' was his sole comment as he lay back against a rock, drawing on a thin stogie.

This was the third coach that the gang had robbed since being formed two months before. The other two heists had netted reasonable takings, though nothing like sufficent to enable them to rest up for a few months. This coach would be different. Pike had learned that it was carrying the monthly payroll for the miners at Sedona Canyon.

Five minutes later a plume of dust rose into the air, heralding the imminent arrival of the coach.

'About goddamned time as well,' huffed Tom Craddock checking his six-shooter.

'Cut with those stogies, boys,' ordered Pike, stepping over to his horse. 'And be ready to ride out when the coach comes round that bend.' He pointed to a huddle of rocks some fifty yards to the west. As soon as they were ready he set his hat straight and said breezily, 'Now fill your hands and let's make us some real dough.'

The rumble of pounding hoofs and thumping

wheels grew louder as the coach drew ever closer. Then suddenly it had rounded the bend. The three men spurred their mounts into the open. Guns blasted into the air.

'Haul up on them leathers, driver,' Roswell shouted, sending another .45 slug buzzing past the old teamster's left ear. It had the desired effect. Neighing and stumbling in their traces, the team of six brought the coach to a juddering halt. Steam rose in clouds from sweating flanks.

'Throw down that twelve-gauge, mister,' ordered Roswell of the guy sitting alongside the driver on the front seat.

But the shotgun guard had other ideas. He pointed his gun at Roswell. The Coyote Kid was the first to react. His Colt blasted twice. Both shots struck the guard in the chest, punching him off the bench. He landed on the hard ground with a dull thud.

Three heads were poked out of the open window, trying to determine what all the ruckus was about.

'Anyone else want to be a hero?' the kid snarled loosing another shell at the wooden coachwork. The heads immediately disappeared. The driver got the message loud and clear. His hands shot skywards.

'Now throw down that strongbox,' snapped Roswell. 'And be quick about it.'

'You're too late, mister,' replied the driver. There was a sneering tone in the guy's voice that irked the gang boss.

'What d'you mean?' Roswell rapped back. 'Too late.'

'Some other jaspers beat you to it. There ain't nothing here to rob save wooden nickles and bent dimes.' The driver couldn't contain himself. Rocking in his seat, he burst out laughing. 'Ha ha ha! Robbed twice in one day. Ain't never happened to me before. Them miners at Sedona ain't gonna be so pleased though. But what a story to tell my grandkids.'

The old-timer's levity was more than Roswell could endure. His own pistol barked until the hammer clicked on to an empty chamber.

'This sure ain't no joke, mulehead,' he railed. 'And you ain't gonna be laughing no more.'

This further volley of shots was too much for the skittish team. The two front runners reared up and the entire team stampeded off down the trail. The gang were left high and dry, staring open-mouthed after the receding coach. Empty-handed and morose, they watched it disappear. Lady Luck had abandoned them. All three were too dejected even to chase off after the stage and at least get something from the passengers.

The Coyote Kid was especially downcast.

'I figured we were going to become rich by teaming up with you, Pike,' he complained, aiming a surly glance at the older man. 'Guess we ain't no better off now than we were before.'

'It weren't my fault that some other outfit got there afore us,' Roswell countered with vigour. 'Anyways, there'll be other jobs. You just have to be a bit more patient like your brother. Ain't that so, Frank?'

The elder Craddock shrugged. This setback had dented his faith in Pike Roswell's ability to make the easy dough he had promised them.

They headed off along the trail in the opposite direction to that taken by the stagecoach. Their heads were slumped on their chests. A downcast spirit imbued the stymied trio.

FOUR

BAD MOVE BY COYOTE

So here they were, camped in a small clearing off the main trail. Staring into the flickering embers of a campfire, they waited morosely while a stringy rabbit roasted.

Pike was racking his brains, trying to work out how best to increase their fortunes. Stagecoaches were easiest to hold up. The problem was that too many other jiggers thought the same. His current situation proved that. Banks, on the other hand, held a lot more dough. Maybe they were their best option. Pike nodded silently to himself.

Coyote broke into his ruminations.

'I'm going down to the creek for some water.'

Nobody looked up. The young outlaw collected the water bottles and slung them over his shoulder. Then he pushed through the tangle of thorny bushes and made his way down to the flowing waters of the Polacca Wash. Approaching the creek, his ears picked up the lilting cadence of a singing voice.

He stopped, unable to comprehend what he was hearing. But there it was, rising and falling in soft tones. And not only that: it was female. He moved closer, gently pushing aside the low branches of dwarf willow that cloaked the water's edge.

Tom Craddock could barely credit what his eyes were telling him.

Bathing in the gentle flow was an Indian girl. The sinuous form swayed to the rhythm of her tribal song as a hand soaped her naked body. Tom felt like emulating the creature whose name he had adopted, but he refrained from giving the coyote howl. Instead he feasted his bulging peepers on the lithe vision of beauty.

For what seemed an age he just stood there, ogling the copper-toned form. His loins ached with lustful thoughts. The young woman's body swayed gently like a leaf in the breeze, presenting a mesmeric sight that had the young outlaw completely enthralled.

Only when the girl ceased her delicate warbling and moved towards the bank did he sink back into the concealment of the shrubbery.

Tom had never seen a more desirable sight in his short life. He intended taking full advantage of the opportunity now presented before he awoke from what had to be a dream.

The squaw had her back to him as he emerged from cover.

He cat-footed across the glade and grabbed her from behind. His gnarled hand snaked around her neck choking off any cry for help. Not that there were any other Indians about, but he didn't want his buddies getting wind of his discovery and muscling in on the act.

Some time later the somewhat dishevelled Coyote Kid stumbled back into the camp.

'You took your time,' observed Frank when his brother belatedly arrived. 'It looks like you got dragged through a bush.'

The Kid's hair was mussed up and his shirt was torn. Streaks of blood dribbled from a scratch on his right cheek. The Indian girl had not willingly succumbed to her tormentor's lecherous fumblings. But nonetheless, a dreamy smile creased his face.

Roswell scrambled to his feet, 'What you been up to, Kid?' he snapped, eyeing the leering kid suspiciously. 'All you went down there for was to fill up the water bottles.'

'Gee, boys,' Tom mumbled, a faraway look in his glazed eyes. 'That gal sure was a wild cat, but stunning all the same.'

The gang boss hurried across. He grabbed the boy roughly by the scruff of the neck and slapped him hard across the mouth. The moony grin instantly disappeared. The Kid's hand dropped to seek the gun on his hip. But Roswell had already snatched it from the holster. It was now jammed into Tom Craddock's stomach.

'You tell us what in thunder you've been up to,'

the gang boss hissed, keeping a firm grip on the kid's shirt front. 'If'n there's a wagon train close by and you've had your way with a settler's daughter—'

'It was only a squaw, Pike, honest,' Tom interjected with an imploring appeal as he cautiously freed himself from the iron grip. 'And she was alone.' The dreamy expression reasserted itself. 'A real beauty.'

'Never mind about that,' rasped the boss. 'What was an Indian girl doing out here alone?'

'Could be she was returning to the tribe,' suggested Frank, 'and just happened to stop for the night by the creek.'

Roswell considered the remark, then cast the kid a rapier-keen look. 'Did you even bother to get her name?' He was a man of the old school who held all those of the opposite sex in respectful esteem, even squaws. 'Or was you in too much of a hurry to. . . .' He couldn't bring himself to complete the accusation.

'She did say that her name was Little White Dove and she was a Navajo.' Tom gingerly fingered a swelling lump on his head. 'That was when she managed to grab a branch and crack me before escaping on her horse.'

Pike took a step back. His own eyes bulged.

'You durned crazy fool!' he exclaimed with scathing contempt. 'Do you know who Little White Dove is?'

Coyote's blank look was enough to show that he had no idea.

'Only the blamed daughter of Shongopovi, chief

39

of the largest tribe in this part of Arizona.'

Roswell threw the foolish youth to the ground. Slamming a bunched fist into the palm of his hand, he angrily stamped around the camp like a bear with a sore head. His dancing shadow cast by the flickering flames of the campfire gave off an aura of menace. He eventually lurched to a halt, jabbing an accusatory finger at the object of his wrath.

'And that critter is one mean-eyed cuss. You've sure gone and dumped us in the midden this time, kid.'

'I-I didn't know,' whined Coyote, his plaintive wail akin to that of his namesake. 'I just saw this vision splashing about in the creek and—'

'We know what you did, Tom,' his brother interrupted, a mite prickly himself at his own kin's foolishness.

'You never damn well thought,' railed Pike.

'What we gonna do now then, boss?' asked Frank Craddock.

'Only thing we can do is get out of here pronto,' replied Roswell. He kicked sand over the fire. 'Once Shongopovi learns that some piece of white trash has violated his daughter, the whole damned tribe will be painting up and heading this way. And it won't be to shake our hands in gratitude. Hang on to your hair, boys, cos that's what they'll be after.'

He threw another withering look of scorn at his young associate. But this was no time for recriminations. They needed to get away, and fast.

*

What Pike Roswell had not counted on was the swiftness of the Navajo chieftain's reaction. Shongopovi wasted no time idly fuming over his daughter's shameful treatment at the hands of the yellow-haired white man after she had arrived back at Canyon de Chelly.

The braves were immediately summoned to prepare themselves for a mission of revenge against the perpetrator. The chief caressed his new long gun. Now it would be able to speak for the tribe by erasing the hurt done to Little White Dove. But more important, it would avenge the dire insult heaped upon the chief and his family. Such a response was expected of a proud leader in order to maintain his authority.

Shongopovi would not disappoint.

Just before the braves chosen for the task left camp, Tocahatchi emerged from the hogan where he had been confined.

Approaching the select group he addressed his father, 'Let me come with you, O Great Chief of the Navajo,' he beseeched with spirit, bowing low before his father, 'so that I may redeem my honour in your eyes and once again ride tall as a true Navajo brave should. It is my sister whose body has been violated at the hands of the hated white eyes. Grant this wish, O wise one, and I will abase myself before the gods of our forefathers in a manner chosen by the tribal elders.'

Shongopovi's leathery features remained devoid of expression. For a long minute he studied the bent head. Then he turned to the elders who had gathered to witness the imminent departure.

'What say you, my brothers?' he asked, the flinty gaze panning the line of wizened elders. 'Should my son's plea be granted? Shongopovi will abide by your decision.'

A low murmuring followed as the tribal council quickly discussed the issue. One of them eventually stepped forward.

'I, Moenkopi, speak for all members of the council.'

He indicated the other tribal elders with a languid arm as he voiced their collective decision in the Navajo tongue.

'We consider that what Tocahatchi asks is unusual, but worthy of merit. Under the circumstances we therefore agree to his proposal.' The council spokesman assumed a more sombre tone when he added, 'But as he himself points out, a humbling task will be expected of him upon the successful completion of your mission.'

The chief nodded. 'Then so be it.'

Tocahatchi heaved a sigh of relief as a brave handed him the reins of his horse. The outcome was far better than he could have expected.

On the following day, Roswell and his two sidekicks were making their way along the dry bed of an arroyo. The cutting was narrow, which necessitated that they travel in single file. So far there had been no sign of any Indians.

But that was about to end.

Frank Craddock was the one who spotted the other line of riders. They were paralleling the direction taken by the outlaws along a ridge some quarter-mile distant on the right. His back stiffened, an edgy movement quickly noted by Roswell.

'Somethin' bugging you, Frank?' he enquired charily.

'Take a look over there, Pike,' the elder Craddock muttered, gesturing to his right.

Roswell shot a glance towards the ridge indicated. He cursed aloud.

'Indians!' He spat out the snappy exclamation as if it were a piece of tough gristle. 'And it looks like they're painted up.'

How long the critters had been there could only be guessed at. They were making no move to hide their presence. They were just out of carbine range and it was clear that they were trying to intimidate the white men.

'Keep your eyes on them, Frank,' he ordered. 'It's only a matter of time before they come a-calling.' His eyes panned the lay of the land ahead. 'What I need is to suss out some place where we can hunker down.'

'Why don't we make a run for it, boss?' queried Tom Craddock in an edgy voice. The stark presence of Indians had clearly had its unnerving effect on one member of the gang.

Roswell snapped back an acid riposte.

'Ain't no chance that these flea-bitten nags can outrun Indian ponies.' He shot a menacing scowl at his young associate. 'It's because of you letting that

43

pecker of your'n do all the thinking, that we'll have to make a stand and hope to fight 'em off. You best start praying, kid, for all our sakes that they ain't packing repeaters.'

They continued along the arroyo for a further ten minutes, the Indians dogging their every step. Then Roswell spotted a clearing surrounded on three sides by ponderosa pine trees. This was just what he had been searching for.

'When I give the word,' he said, levelling an arm towards the tree cover, 'ride like old Nick himself was tickling your ass.'

He gave a quick glance to assure himself that the Indians had not likewise spotted the sheltering arbour, then he shouted, 'Let's go, boys!'

Spurs dug deep into the flanks of the three mounts. Startled by the sudden jolt, the horses snickered fearfully, then bounded forward, urged on by slapping leathers. The fugitives hugged their necks. Nobody risked a look towards the ridge. Their attention was purely focused on reaching the cover offered by the small copse of trees.

After what seemed like a hour, in fact little more than two minutes, the horses floundered to a halt in a welter of dust. Their riders leapt from the saddle, grabbing rifles, and hurled themselves behind the cover afforded by some fallen pine trunks.

They had been none too soon. A minute later the pounding of hoofs assailed their ears.

The line of Indians galloped through the glade, searching for their prey.

'OK, boys, here they come,' yelled a thoroughly animated Pike Roswell, the blood hammering inside his head. 'Make every shot count.'

Fresh rounds were loaded into the Winchesters. Rounding a bend, the leading Indian received the full force of hot lead as the rifles blasted. Another was also quickly punched off the back of his pony.

Whooping and hollering, the surviving braves continued with their thundering charge. But the raucous display was a ploy intended to unsettle their adversaries.

As one, the remainder slid over the sides of their mounts, knees tightly hugging the flanks. At the same time a flurry of arrows was loosed at the gun-flashes from beneath the horses' necks: a trick that few white men had ever been able to perfect.

However, the sudden rattle of gunfire had caught the Indians unawares, which sent their aim awry. Consequently, none of the arrows found their marks. The outlaws replied with more rifle fire. But with no visible targets, the pursuing bullets whistled harmlessly by overhead.

At the far end of the corridor, the Indians wheeled about to regroup and made ready for another charge. A third brave tumbled out of the saddle. But on this occasion the aim of those remaining was far more accurate. Frank Craddock's hat was lifted from his head.

Before he had a chance to recover from the near miss another Indian flung himself from his galloping horse on to the stunned outlaw. Frank saw the lunging knife in the nick of time. It hissed past his head, the razor-sharp point burying itself in a nearby log.

The outlaw quickly recovered from the sudden assault. But Frank was no knife-fighter. A six-shooter was his weapon of choice. The Smith & Wesson Schofield leapt into his hand. Two bullets terminated the brief contest.

His brother yelped in pain as an arrow scored a furrow across his upper arm. It was only a flesh wound, but enough to send the young tough huddling down behind the protection afforded by a tree trunk. More arrows twanged into the timber. The close proximity of the lethal barbs had a disturbing effect on the trio.

Roswell knew that he was lucky to have escaped injury. Gripping the Winchester in his sweating hands he continued firing, the barrel growing hot to his touch. Lever, aim and fire! Lever, aim and fire! Desperation lent speed to reflex action until the gun clicked on empty.

The gang's furious defence of their small redoubt, however, was enough to drive the attackers back. But only temporarily.

At that moment the sharp crack of a rifle sounded from the end of the clearing. A second shot followed moments later. Slivers of bark showered the cowering outlaws. Roswell's worst fear had come to pass.

At least one of the Indian band had a repeater. The gang was safe for the moment. But for how long?

The Indians had fallen silent. They did not make

any further attempts at a frontal assault.

Fifteen minutes passed.

'D'you think they've given up?' the kid squawked nervously.

Roswell gave that notion a derisive snort. 'You sure ain't got no idea about Indians, have you, kid?' he sneered. 'Only way they'll give up is if'n we kill 'em all, or they kill us.'

'How many do you figure there are, Pike?' enquired Frank scanning the clearing for any movement that might indicate how the Indians intended to proceed.

Roswell gave the question serious consideration. 'Can't have been more than a dozen out there. We've reduced that by three. So maybe nine are left. Still not good odds, though.'

Shadows were creeping across the landscape as the day drew to a close.

'D-do Indians attack at night?' stuttered a jittery Tom Craddock, his eyes flicking about nervously.

'Far as I know, most Indians reckon that evil spirits wander around after dark. They stick close to a fire to avoid meeting up with any bad ju-ju,' offered Roswell, rolling himself a stogie. He lit up and drew the smoke deep into his lungs. 'Let's hope that Navajo are no different.'

'If'n that's the case then we oughta be able to sneak away from here after sundown,' said Frank Craddock.

'That's my thinking as well,' concurred Roswell. 'And if'n we can get off their lands, just maybe they'll decide to call it a day and leave us alone.' He was trying to inject some positive thinking into their situation. Although in truth, he was not confident of their being let off the hook.

An hour later a dull glow could be seen through the trees.

'Looks like them Indians have set up camp over yonder,' observed Frank.

'We'll give them another half-hour to settle down, then make our move,' Roswell decided. 'Meanwhile keep your eyes peeled, just in case they ain't bothered by any bad spirits.'

The sun had disappeared behind the dark ramparts of the distant mountains when the three outlaws led their mounts silently out of the small grove of trees.

They placed hands over the horses' muzzles to prevent them snickering and thus alerting the Indians. Thankfully, Lady Luck had backed their play. Once at a safe distance they mounted up and headed off.

Only when they were certain that the Indians were not following did the tension ease. But Roswell was not for stopping. He intended putting as much distance as possible between the gang and their pursuers.

FIVE

PURSUIT

All through the night they kept up a gentle pace.

The sky remained cloudless. A silvery moon offered an ethereal glow to guide the riders across the broken terrain. There was no chance of stretching the horses to a full gallop, but a steady canter soon ate up the miles. The greater the distance that Roswell put between himself and the vengeful Navajos, the more he could relax.

Dawn breaking over the Sitareave mountains brought a welcome relief to the tired men.

They had ridden non-stop all through the night. A pink and mauve skyscape heralded the new day's rising. After cresting a low knoll the gang leader drew to a halt. He screwed up his tired eyes and squinted back along the way they had come, nervously scanning the landscape for any signs of pursuit.

Nothing. The arid wilderness appeared devoid of life. Yet even in this unforgiving land, life was played out in all its tenuous forms.

Overhead, a bald eagle flew over the new horizon. It circled high on the early morning thermals, relentlessly searching for its breakfast. The gently floating bundle of feathers drifted with easy grace, its dark shape silhouetted against the rapidly strengthening light of day.

Then suddenly the bird dropped like a stone. A squeal followed. A successful catch. The bird lifted off the ground, a desert rat clutched in its hooked talons. The gang boss swallowed. He prayed that the Indians would not likewise catch their prey unawares.

'Any chance of a break, boss?' moaned Coyote. 'My ass is rubbing somethin' awful.'

'Five minutes and no more,' rapped Roswell. 'The relay station at Bitter Creek is on the far side of Window Rock.' He pointed to a prominent excrescence of red sandstone through which the wind had scoured a large hole. 'I'll feel a heap safer when we reach it.'

The kid gingerly lifted his stiff body from the saddle. Waddling around, he looked like a lame duck. The bizarre sight brought some relief to his sidekicks, if not to him, as they chortled uproariously at his discomfort.

'What's so funny?' grumbled the kid, rubbing at his nether regions.

'You'd sure know if you was sitting where I am,' Pike hooted with glee. Frank couldn't help but join in the jovial banter.

The mirthful incident allowed Roswell's tense muscles to ease up. By noon they would be out of Navajo territory. Then they could change horses at the relay station. Feeling buoyed up, he magnanimously allowed the kid an extra ten minutes to ease his aching butt. At the same time Frank changed the rough dressing on his brother's wounded arm.

Pike himself could have used a hot mug of strong coffee and some vittles, but there was not enough time for that. Nor did he want rising smoke to give their position away to any eagle-eyed Indians. They would have to make do with tepid water and hard tack. A cigar, however, helped to smooth out the tightness in his limbs.

Around noon they hit the main stagecoach trail. The relay station couldn't be far now.

'Looks like we made it, boys,' yipped the upbeat gang leader.

'I could sure use a bath and some decent grub,' said Frank with a sigh. His fertile brain was conjuring up a steaming-hot tub followed by a mammoth steak and fried potatoes. 'Beats your trail grub any day.'

The offhand remark aimed at Roswell's culinary abilities was received with ribald good humour.

'You sure do need that bath. Frank,' Pike countered blithely. 'A skunk would turn its nose up at your smell.'

'He's right there, brother,' agreed the kid, holding his nose, the tenderness of his hindquarters all but forgotten.

The three of them were riding in line along the well-worn trail. With the threat to their lives now well to their rear, the sombre mood of fear had been lifted. What they did not realize was that Shongopovi was not about to give up his quest so easily.

The Navajo was a grimly determined foe. He was well-known for doggedly pursuing a quarry until satisfaction for any slight had been achieved.

He had certainly not yet achieved satisfaction for the slight upon his daughter.

With three men dead, the chief was now more than ever intent on exacting a full and convincing retribution. Only the spilling of white blood would realize that end. And any other white eyes they encountered would meet with the same fate. His braves and their families expected no less of their chief.

The Indians were expert trackers. The cloudless night had been their friend, enabling then to follow the clear trail left by the gang with ease.

As they neared the relay station at Bitter Creek, so Pike and his sidekicks had eased their pace. This had allowed the pursuing Indians to catch up. Keeping a suitable distance in the rear, Shongopovi waited until he could approach close enough for a surprise and, this time, decisive attack.

The meandering trail that twisted and turned between fractured turrets of rock enabled the Indians to manoeuvre to within a hundred yards of their quarry without fear of being spotted. Not that the gang had bothered to keep an eye on their back trail, so confident were they of being out of danger.

It therefore came as a total surprise when the blood-curdling battle cry erupted just behind them.

Whooping and hollering, Shongopovi and his remaining band appeared round the bend in a cloud of dust. A deputation from hell come to avenge their fallen comrades in a bloody reprisal. Arrows zipped around the startled trio.

One buried itself in the neck of Frank Craddock's horse. Though not a fatal wound, the animal reared up, throwing its rider to the ground. Blood poured from the puncture as it bolted into the surrounding huddle of rocks leaving its rider to flounder helplessly.

Roswell was the first to recover from the shock. With a deft drag on the reins, he wrestled his own cayuse around.

'Up here, Frank!' he yelled above the din, leaning over to grab the fallen man's raised arm. In a single fluid motion, Frank was hauled off the ground on to the back of Roswell's horse. Thankful arms encircled his saviour's torso.

While all this was happening the younger Craddock stood his ground. He loosed off a couple of rapid-fire shots from his rifle to deter the vengeful pursuers. A whoop of triumph followed as one of them tumbled off his horse. The swift response had the desired effect of slowing down Shongopovi's manic charge.

'OK, boys,' hollered Roswell, with Frank now clinging on behind. 'Time we was out of here.'

Digging his spurs into the flanks of his mount, he galloped away with Coyote close behind. A couple of shots from the temporarily thwarted Navajo chief buzzed around their heads.

Frank knew that the relay station was not far distant. He also knew that a horse carrying two men could not maintain the fast pace for long. The Indians had only temporarily been held off.

Already he could hear their cries of pursuit. The kid dispatched a few bullets from his revolver back down the trail, more from desperation than with any hope of stopping the Indians.

Ten minutes passed. Roswell's horse was tiring fast. Its frenetic gallop had slowed to a stumbling jog. No amount of crazed urging could gain the extra speed.

The gang boss risked a brief glance over his shoulder. The Indians were drawing much closer than he had thought.

Angry shouts sounding like a pack of rabid dogs rang in his ears. Any second now the red devils would be within arrow range. A bullet zipped past his head. He felt the wind of its passing. Panic lent urgency to his efforts to spur the drained horse to increase its pace.

As they rounded a stand of cottonwoods the wooden buildings of the Bitter Creek complex came in view. A sanctuary, a welcoming haven, an oasis of safety.

But were they too late?

SIX

OMINOUS REUNION

Madison was leaning against the kitchen doorjamb watching Eleanor Newbold. It was a sight that made him feel somewhat guilty. She was helping to wash up the dishes following their midday meal. He casually lit a cigar while studying the lithe form of his latest commitment.

The swaying hips had him transfixed. The object of his admiration was completely unaware that she was being thus admired. Bearclaw did not enlighten her. He was enjoying the comely spectacle.

There was no doubting that she sure was a handsome female. Any man worth his salt would move heaven and earth to get such a winsome creature back. But of Howard Thompson there had been no word according to Kingman. The image of his wife once more swam before Bat's rheumy eyes, raising the notion that he ought not be harbouring such lascivious thoughts.

More practical matters, however, reasserted themselves. He had not heard tell of any other search
being mounted. His shoulders lifted. Maybe that was
because he had more experience in these matters
and knew the score when it came to a executing such
a rescue.

Whatever the case, Eleanor would be leaving the
next day on the Albuquerque stage and that would
be the end of another wild-goose chase. These idle
speculations were interrupted by a call from outside.

'Care to give me a hand, Mr Madison?'

It was an unspoken understanding that stagecoach
passengers and other guests at relay stations under-
took various tasks in exchange for their board and
lodging. The manager was reimbursed by the
company for any expenses incurred by taking in
guests for the night.

The normal procedure was for the women to
handle the household chores while the men helped
around the buildings, doing any jobs that were
deemed necessary. Madison had chopped a pile of
wood for the cooking fire that morning.

The stagecoach was late arriving. He had hoped to
see his charge safely on her way back to Albuquerque
before departing himself. It was looking like they
would have to remain at the station for another
night.

He wasn't worried. Coaches were often late. It
might be that a flooded river had necessitated a
detour. Or maybe a broken axle. On two occasions
he had ridden in a coach where a lame horse in the

team had slowed progress to little more than a walk.

He levered himself off the doorpost and quietly sidled away.

Outside in the front yard Chet Kingman had grasped hold of a long-handled axe. He nodded to its double, which was leaning against the thick stump of an old ponderosa.

'This old boy has been taking up valuable space in the yard for long enough,' he declared, taking hold of the axe. 'The two of us working together could shift it in an hour.'

It was a statement rather than a request for assistance. Nonetheless, there was a challenging gleam in the manager's eye that questioned whether this guy was up to such physical labour.

Madison met his gaze with a regard of lofty assurance. Slowly he peeled off his dark-blue shirt to reveal a torso of rippling corded muscle. He folded the blue flannel shirt up and placed it to one side with his hat. Then, in a single smoothly executed motion, he hefted the axe above his head and swung it down hard at the base of the tree. Chips of wood flew off as Kingman quickly joined him.

In no time they had established a steady rhythm. Sharpened blades bit deep as heavy clunks echoed across the yard in measured tempo. No words were uttered as each man applied himself to his task. None were needed.

Mango, the station wolfhound, stopped chasing his tail to watch the strange contest, the winner being he who took the first breather. Neither the men nor the beast realized that this particular trial of strength would not be completed.

They were halfway through when the sound of gunfire assaulted their ears. It was accompanied by the all too familiar cries of attacking Indians. The contest was immediately forgotten as both men paused in their exertions. Together they looked towards the direction from which the spine-tingling hoots were coming.

'Indians!' hollered Kingman, throwing the axe down. It was a reflex exclamation that needed no questioning. Neither did his next comment. Madison was already hustling over to the barn for his revolver. 'Grab your gun, Bat. Looks like we're under attack!'

Sheltering behind the well, Bat cocked his pistol and made ready to cut loose when the Indians came into view. His startled eyes widened on seeing three white men galloping ahead of the pursuing braves.

The welter of dust made it difficult to see who was who. All of a sudden, out of the swirling cloud, a rider emerged. He dived off his mount and scuttled behind a nearby cluster of hay bales. The other two followed in quick succession.

Seconds later the first Indians appeared, their faces painted up, and sporting war feathers. Knees gripping their ponies, the Indians loosed a rapid salvo of arrows towards their quarry. Guns responded with venomous anger. One Indian screamed. Throwing up his arms, he tumbled from his horse.

Another launched himself at Bat, who was too busy taking aim at the chief whom he recognized as the intimidating Shongopovi. A scowl creased his sweat-stained features as he also noted the rifle that the Indian leader was arrogantly waving aloft. A vengeful imprecation rumbled in his throat as his finger tightened on the trigger.

But a sneaky Indian got his attack in first.

Bat was flung to the ground. His gun was knocked out of his hand, spinning away out of reach. He lay spread-eagled on his stomach and stunned from the attack; his mouth gaped wide as the Indian came at him. Bearclaw Madison's end had surely come.

The pair locked eyes, the Indian howling with triumph as he fell upon his helpless victim. His knife hand rose to deliver the *coup de grâce*. Its deadly blade glinted in the sunlight. Bat watched it descend as if in slow motion, helpless to avert the inevitable.

Then another shot rang out close by. It stopped the would-be killer in his tracks. Arms thrown skywards, back arched like a bow, the brave tottered over his prey then keeled sideways into the dust.

With two more of his braves down, Shongopovi knew that the odds were stacked against him. The chief's arms circled windmill fashion, as he shouted out an order to retreat. Bullets pursued the fleeing braves as they disappeared into the swirling yellow dust.

Bat breathed deep. His heart was pounding fit to burst. That had been the closest he had ever come to cashing in his chips. For a long minute he just lay on the ground. Then he saw a shadow. A man loomed over him, blotting out the sun. A gnarled hand reached down. He grasped it. Dragged to his feet, Bat mumbled a weak 'thank you' to his saviour.

And that was when he received another shock.

'It's been a long time, Bat,' Roswell said, handing his old buddy his shirt and hat. 'Must be all of five years.'

Bat nodded his thanks as he dusted himself down. Before he had time to utter a response the Craddock boys appeared beside their leader.

'Boy, that was a close shave,' gasped Tom thumbing fresh shells into the loading slot of his carbine. 'We only just made it. And those nags are plumb tuckered out. Mine's keeled over. Reckon I'm gonna have to finish him off.'

The remark was ignored as the two old associates continued to look each other over.

'You hear me, Pike?' repeated the kid. 'I said that—'

Roswell raised a hand, cutting short the young man's words. 'Seems like I keep making a habit of saving your hide,' he said to Bat. Then, in a more menacing tone, he added, 'Pity you didn't have the same consideration towards me.'

Frank Craddock's brow furrowed as he looked from his leader to the stranger. 'You two fellas know each other?' he asked.

'We surely do, boys, and that's a fact.' Roswell shrugged off any animosity he might have felt towards his old partner. He paused, holding the guy with a sly grimace. 'Ain't that so, Bat?' A hand reached out to handle the necklace of bear claws. 'I see this lucky charm is still working its magic.'

At last Bat was able to find his own voice.

'Let's go inside and talk about this over some coffee,' he mumbled. He turned to lead the way into the station.

Roswell nodded, then addressed his two associates.

'You boys see to the horses.' A caustic eye fastened on to the kid. 'And if'n you have to do the business with that nag, make sure the lady don't see.' He nodded towards Eleanor Newbold, who had just emerged from the kitchen. Even wearing an old apron and with her hair all awry there was no denying that she commanded attention. She received it in full measure from Pike Roswell.

'Sure thing, boss,' replied Coyote. He led the tired horse away.

'And keep your eyes peeled for them Indians coming back,' the gang boss added. He then slapped Madison on the back. 'Me and old Bat here have some catching up to do.'

The grin that spread across the outlaw's steely features was of an icy quality. To a close observer he appeared anything but affable. There was clearly a history shared by these two old associates.

The object of Roswell's friendly attention was quickly recovering from his unnerving experience. The sudden and totally unexpected appearance of an old comrade had brought a whole parcel of memories flooding back.

They were not all pleasant, either. Not by a long chalk.

SEVEN

INCIDENT AT LAWRENCE

Bat's association with Roswell had begun in 1864, towards the end of the Civil War between the Union and the Confederacy. They were members of a guerilla detachment known as the Border Ruffians, one of many such groups operating across the arena of conflict.

The Border Ruffians were headed by an ex-farmer whose holding had been destroyed in one of the blue-belly purges. A neutral stance had quickly developed into an all-consuming hatred for the Northern cause. The best way to vent his passion against the enemy was by means of covert operations. Hit the target hard, then disappear quickly. The Ruffians became will-o'-the-wisps who struck fear into the enemy.

As a consequence, the name of Sabretooth Jack Strype became synonymous with terror. The operations were on a small scale to begin with, but the punishing attacks soon grew into major thorns in the side of their adversaries. Such was the success of the Ruffians that Union commanders felt impotent against their depredations.

It was late afternoon: the best time to make a successful hit. There would be a full day's takings at a time when the bank was about to close its doors for the day.

Strype held up a warning hand. The ten riders behind slowed to a halt.

The Ruffians were outside the Kansas town of Lawrence where, two years previously, another band under the famous William Clarke Quantrill had exacted a bloody revenge in which many of the town's citzens had been killed.

Strype had no intention of repeating that vengeful attack. His objective was profit only. The bank in Lawrence was known to hold serious reserves of cash used to pay the Union forces operating in Kansas.

Acquisition of the loot was not meant for personal gain. It was intended to distribute the money among those who had suffered most from enemy activity. Commandeering the regular receipts, however, would be an added bonus for the men.

The Wardle Bank was situated in the centre of the town in a plaza where four roads converged. The gang would ride in separately along the eastern concourse, positioning themselves at different points around the plaza. On Strype's signal, those selected to assist with the heist would casually amble across while two men looked after the horses.

'You all know what to do.' It was a statement of fact, not intended for discussion. Strype speared the hovering riders with a caustic gaze. Nobody made to reply. 'Check your hardware.' There was a sound of rustling as hands withdrew pistols and the ten Ruffians snapped the hammers to half-cock. Cylinders buzzed as they were spun to reveal fully loaded chambers. 'OK, boys, let's go rob us a bank.'

A sharp intake of breath sounded as the band moved forward.

Pike Roswell nudged his buddy with an elbow.

'This one should be a piece of cake,' he said with a leery grin. 'And this time we get to eat some of it.' He chuckled at his own wit.

'About time as well is what I say,' replied Bat Madison. 'Them sodbusters have done a sight better out of this war than us.'

'At least your folks got to rebuild their spread proper-like,' observed Roswell in a somewhat aggrieved tone. 'Mine were only able to buy fresh seed and a new milking cow. Pa had to make do with a one-roomed soddy after that bastard Grant had destroyed everything with his policy of total annihilation.' A snarl rumbled in his throat.

'Cut the talk back there,' rapped Strype. 'Save it for when the job's done.'

Jack Strype had persuaded his superiors that

guerilla tactics would help considerably in undermining Northern morale. He had formed the Border Ruffians after relinquishing his command of a mounted regiment. He controlled them with military precision. That was the reason they had become so successful: a force to be reckoned with in the deadly conflict.

Soft afternoon sunlight glinted on the burnished steel of a cavalry sabre clutched in Strype's left hand, He now pointed the weapon forward. It was as if he was about to make a charge against enemy lines.

The blade was Strype's constant companion and it had given him the chilling nickname of Sabretooth. It was the only part of his equipment that signified an affiliation to the Confederate cause.

A tense silence descended over the line of riders as they moved off down a shallow grade towards the edge of the town. After splitting up into pairs, they circled around to approach the plaza along the various roads. As a result, nobody gave the newcomers a second glance.

Fifteen minutes later the men were in position.

Strype idly lounged against the wall at the side of the bank. His beady eyes flicked about. Satisfied that all was as it should be, he raised his hat, revealing a shock of curly brown hair, and scratched his head. That was the signal that the job was on.

Instantly the nine figures scattered about the square tensed. Casually the robbers led their mounts to a prescribed hitching rail, then joined Strype. A quick glance around to determine their actions had passed without notice and the lethargic movements disappeared. They were now precise and determined, a well-trained force of veteran combatants.

In the shake of a rat's tail they were inside the bank.

Being the last man inside, Pike Roswell locked the outer door and pulled down the blind.

'Everybody stay where they are,' Strype commanded in a strident tone that brooked no dissent, 'Do as you're told and nobody will be harmed.'

The men were ranged out behind him and to his sides. Ice-cold glares matched the cocked pistols aimed at the three startled men on the far side of the counter. The abrupt appearance of the robbers completely transfixed the bank clerks. Like rabbits under the gaze of a swaying sidewinder, they were totally mesmerized.

Only when the leader spoke did they show signs of comprehension.

'You have been granted a visit by the Border Ruffians,' Strype rapped out, regarding the browbeaten tellers with disdain.

Drawing his sabre, he then proceeded to chop hunks of wood from the counter. The brutally ruthless deed was intended to intimidate: it had always worked thus far. This was to be no exception.

Satisfied that he had their full and undivided cooperation, Strype then continued: 'We are commandeering all funds held in this bank for use by the Confederate cause.' He flung two empty flour sacks over the counter. 'Fill these up with notes only.'

Within five minutes the bags were stuffed full. But there was still some dough left over. 'Fill your pockets, boys,' breezed the gang leader. 'No sense leaving anything behind.' He bestowed a leery smile upon the cowering clerks. 'Then we'd have to come back.'

At that moment a door at the rear of the office opened and the manager emerged holding a Smith & Wesson .38 in each hand. Without uttering a word he began firing indiscriminately. Bullets flew everywhere. The three clerks hit the floor as glass shattered and chunks of splintered wood flew everywhere.

One of the robbers spun as a bullet struck him in the chest. He went down and remained still.

The other robbers quickly recovered from this unexpected resistance. Their own weapons exploded in volleys of hot lead. Their adversary backed away, trying to find cover. He might have made it had not one of his guns jammed and the other clicked empty.

A howl of triumph erupted from the mouths of the robbers. Thier antagonist went down in a hail of gunfire.

'A brave though foolish man,' observed Strype, backing towards the door. 'Much obliged to the rest of you but I think it's time for us to leave.' His voice rose to a stentorian yell. 'That racket will have woken the devil himself. Let's hightail it, boys.'

He dashed outside. On hearing the gunfire within, the two wranglers had hurriedly brought the horses to the front door of the bank. Already, concerned citizens were emerging from the buildings around the plaza to discover what had caused the uproar. On witnessing their savings being stolen, shouts of outrage greeted the robbers as they slammed out of the bank.

Bullets began to fly thick and fast.

The alarmed desperadoes dug in their spurs and galloped off along the westbound thoroughfare. Hot lead pursued them down the street like a horde of angry wasps. Bent low, the robbers hugged the necks of their horses, urging them onward to greater speed.

After fifty yards, the highway veered to the right, effectively blocking the aim of the incensed citizens of Lawrence. The Ruffians pounded onwards, anxious to get well away from the scene of their latest iniquity.

All except one.

At the corner, on the verge of reaching safety, a bullet struck Bat Madison's cayuse. He was the last rider. So none of the others saw the animal stumble, then pitch over on to its back, throwing its rider into the dust.

Madison hit the ground hard. But panic at being left behind by his buddies stirred in him a manic will to survive. Lurching to his feet, he hollered at the top of his voice.

'Pike! Pike! Don't leave me here!'

The desperate plea struck home. Pike Roswell had been just ahead of his sidekick. Risking a look behind, he saw his buddy waving his arms like a demented scarecrow.

Roswell did not hesitate. He hauled violently on the reins, jerking his horse around with a drummimg of stomping hoofs. Then he galloped back up the street at full pelt, his left arm bent like a hook and held out stiffly.

Madison breathed deeply positioning himself to execute the rescue manoeuvre known as the Missouri lock. His arm was flexed in a similar manner. The gang had practised this acrobatic method of pick-up for just such an eventuality as this. He would only be granted the one chance before the irate citizens of Lawrence rounded the bend and blasted him into the hereafter.

As Roswell drew closer he made to approach his buddy in a wide arc down one side of the street, so as to maintain his momentum. This was the first time they had carried out the lock for real.

At the critical moment both arms clashed together. Madison was hooked off the street and on to the back of Roswell's horse. The animal completed the circuit by galloping back up the far side of the street to rejoin the gang, none of whom were aware of what had just occurred.

Only when Jack Strype signalled a halt some thirty minutes later did the gang learn of the rescue.

'What happened to you?' enquired the startled commander when he observed the two backmarkers riding double.

Roswell filled him in. 'Bat here had his nag shot from under him. I couldn't just leave the poor sap afoot to face that mob, could I?'

Strype nodded. A look of approval crossed his grim visage.

'I wouldn't have expected anything less from a member of the Border Ruffians. We'll have to get Bat a fresh mount from the next farm we pass.'

Only a few months later the surrender was signed by Lee and Grant at Appomatox. With the war over, most of the guerilla bands split up to go their separate ways. But there were some commanders who refused to accept that the South had been beaten.

Sabretooth Jack Strype was one such individual, though it was more for the excitement and prospect of easy money that he urged his followers to join him. Strype had no wish to resume the back-breaking toil of homesteading. Pike Roswell was one who heeded the call.

Bat, on the other hand, had experienced his fill of killing and looting. It had been legitimate during the military conflict. To continue would be wrong and would turn the perpetrators into nought but a band of lawless brigands. He had no wish to follow the owlhoot trail. He voiced his feelings in no uncertain manner.

Indeed, Bat Madison had his sights set on upholding the law by becoming a town marshal. So, in the spring of 1865, the Border Ruffians parted company on somewhat acrimonious terms, all going their separate ways.

Inside the cabin, Eleanor poured the two old associates some coffee.

Roswell cast his admiring gaze over the woman's sleek contours. 'And who might this lovely lady be?' he asked, accepting a slice of fresh-baked apple pie while doffing his hat with an exaggerated flourish.

Before Eleanor could reply Bat interjected with a blunt statement. 'I'm waiting here with Miss Newbold to ensure that she catches the Albuquerque stage safely. It should have been here at noon.' He didn't go into details about the abduction and his part in the rescue.

Roswell consulted his pocket watch. 'Seems like it's running a mite late.'

The outlaw didn't bother to enlighten Bat that only a miracle would see the arrival of the stage-coach, its driver and guard having cashed in their chips. Nor did he provide any explanation as to why the Indians were out for the gang's blood. Not that he needed to. Indians and the white men did not make for a palatable mix.

But the name of Newbold had certainly piqued his curiosity. His studied regard of the lady became a frank enquiry.

'You wouldn't by any chance happen to be the betrothed of a certain wealthy rancher from that part of the territory, who was kidnapped by the Navajo?'

Eleanor's satin features displayed her obvious surprise that this man was aware of the kidnapping.

Roswell smiled. 'Everybody in the territory knows about it,' he informed the shocked lady. Then he turned to his old partner. 'So that's why you've taken on the job of chaperon, eh Bat?' He shook his head in mock admonishment. 'Might have known you couldn't kick over the traces completely.'

'What you getting at, Pike?'

Roswell laughed, but the apparent hilarity lacked any degree of warmth. 'Don't play the innocent with me, old buddy. I know you too well. It's the money, ain't it?' He paused for Bat's reaction. But none was forthcoming. So he added with a biting inflection, 'Only the ten big ones that her fiancé has promised to whoever brings the lady back safe and sound.'

Now it was Bat's turn to register surprise.

'I don't know anything about a reward,' he averred firmly.

'And the moon's made of green cheese,' scoffed Roswell. His next cutting remark was aimed at Eleanor. 'If'n you believe that, lady, you ain't the smart cookie I figured you for.'

Eleanor threw a frosty look towards her rescuer. With a deliberate lift of the shoulders, she turned her back on him and abruptly left the room.

Madison was seething. He hadn't even been accorded the chance to deny the accusation. He gritted his teeth impotently. It took a supreme effort to remain calm and detached.

Trouble was, the woman had got under his skin. Roswell hadn't helped by making an acerbic comment just to rub salt in the wound.

The outlaw boss sucked in his breath. 'Seems like you've been leading the lady on.' He smirked through a mouthful of pie crumbs. 'And it sure don't look as if she's too pleased.'

There was no point in Madison denying all knowledge of the reward posted for the woman's return. Nobody would believe him now, least of all Eleanor Newbold. Angrily pushing back his chair, he headed for the door. Anywhere to stop him from causing ructions by brawling with this ogre from the past.

'Serves you damn well right ... *old buddy.*' Roswell's taunts had struck home. The strong emphasis on their past relationship was meant as a deliberate provocation. 'Goes some way to easing the pain I suffered on that chain gang cos of your damned high-and-mighty pride.'

It worked.

Bat paused in the open doorway. Struggling to hold himself in check, he turned around slowly. 'You brought that on all by your lonesome, *old buddy.*' The bitter riposte hissed out. 'Fact is, I saved you from a certain hanging. If'n all that hoorrahing in the Whiplash saloon had continued, sure as eggs is eggs you'd have killed someone.'

Not waiting for a reply, he closed the door on the snarling outlaw.

Once again the events leading up to Pike Roswell's sentence sprang to the forefront of his thoughts. A man does not forget six months hard labour on one of the infamous Kansas chain gangs in a hurry. Pike Roswell was not a forgiving sort of guy.

Absently playing with the bearclaw necklace, Bat Madison lit a cigar. The plume of blue smoke was ejected a tad more forcefully than usual. Blank eyes looked towards some indeterminate point in the distance. From here on, he was going to have to watch his step – and his back.

EIGHT

TROUBLE IN ABILENE

Following the break-up of the Ruffians, Bat drifted west.

He found work that complemented his earlier career, riding shotgun for the Overland stage operating between Tipton and Santa Fe. Since its inception earlier in the century, this lucrative means of trading goods and services with the Mexican authorities had burgeoned considerably. A regular weekly service now connected all towns along the route.

It was during one particular stop-over in the booming cattle town of Abilene, Kansas, that Bat found himself inside the company office. It was early evening. The recently installed street oil-lamps had just been lit.

One of Bat's duties involved acting as guard to the agent when valuable cargo was being handled. In this case it was gold bullion being loaded into a strong-box for transfer to the office in Santa Fe. Bat stood by. A shotgun rested in the crook of his arm as he silently watched the agent check the number of ingots he had received from the bank.

Herby Alcock gave a satisfied nod. 'All present and correct,' he said, ticking off the final slab of yellow metal.

After signing the invoice he slipped it into the heavy iron box and slammed the lid down. The agent's face glistened with sweat in the dim light. Lifting slabs of gold was heavy work. 'Figure I need a drink after that,' he panted, wiping his round face with a necker. 'Fancy joining me in the Cow Palace?' he asked his fellow employee.

'Watching you do all that heavy lifting sure helps to work up a thirst, Herby,' Bat joshed, trying unsuccessfully to keep a straight face. 'I'll just get the strongbox key from the back office. Then we can get it padlocked and safely tucked away in the safe until morning.'

No sooner was he out of sight than the front door burst open.

Three masked men rushed in. They were all carrying guns whch were pointed at Herby Alcock.

'Raise your hands, mister,' growled one of the bandits. 'This is a stick-up. One false move and you're crowbait.'

Another of the men moved across to the strongbox and raised the lid. He pave a low whistle at the hypnotic sight of the metal within. 'All here, Sabretooth,' were the magic words.

Jack Strype grunted with satisfaction. His trade-mark curved sword prodded the agent's bulging stomach. 'Didn't I tell you boys to stick with me if'n you wanted to get rich?' he crowed. 'All we have to do now is carry the box out the back way and load it on to the wagon. Nobody will be any the wiser until morning. By then we'll be long gone.'

The other two laughed as they each grasped one of the rope handles.

But what they hadn't counted on was the presence of another adversary. Bat had disappeared at just the right moment. Seconds later and he would have been caught wrong-footed. Thankfully, the advantage was now in his hands.

Hearing the nickname of his old commander was a shock, although really no surprise under the circumstances. Strype had given his old comrades due notice of which direction he intended taking after the recent hostilties had ended.

Listening on the far side of the rear door, Bat quickly figured out how to stymie this surprise robbery. His plan demanded instant action. Heavy boots were already sounding at the far side of the door. Gauging it just right was imperative.

As the door began to open he slammed a raised boot into it. The sudden jolt wrenched the door back into the men behind. Caught off balance holding the heavy box, they tumbled backwards on to the floor.

Bat stepped forward, shotgun in one hand, his six-shooter in the other.

There was no time for more than an urgent shout to his colleague.

'On the floor, Herby!'

Then the shotgun let rip. An ear-splitting roar shook the building. Flame and smoke poured from both barrels. Taken completely by surprise, the man standing behind the fallen robbers stood no chance. Jack Strype was lifted bodily off his feet by the lethal blast. A large ragged hole blossomed on his chest. The sword clattered on to the floor.

There was no need to check whether he was dead.

The Navy Colt swung to cover the floundering duo. 'On your feet, boys,' rapped the guard. 'Any move towards those pistols and you join old Sabretooth in the hereafter.'

Hands raised, the two brigands scrambled to their feet. Shock at seeing their old comrade on the other end of the lethal shooter stunned them both into silence.

'Before we march you pair of critters over to the jailhouse,' said Bat, 'You can deposit that strongbox back in the safe where it belongs. It'll save old Herby a job.' He looked across to the waxy face of his associate. 'Sure looks like you could use that drink now, Herby,' he announced, suppressing a smile.

'More than one after this,' gasped the shocked agent, desperately trying to calm his trembling body.

Bat then turned his attention back to the robbers.

'Seems like you boys chose the wrong trail in following Sabretooth. What happened to Pike Roswell?'

One of the forlorn bandits provided the answer. 'He decided to head for Texas and try his luck in the cattle business.'

'A wise choice,' remarked Bat grimly. He ushered the two men outside.

The following morning, as Bat was readying himself to continue the stagecoach journey, he was approached by the marshal of Abilene.

'Mind if'n I have a word?' Steel-eye Sam Bannock asked.

'I told you everything I know last night, marshal,' replied Bat making to step up on to the front bench seat of the coach. 'Ain't nothing more I can add. I rode with Strype and those others in the Border Ruffians during the war. After the surrender he and some of the gang went their way. I went mine. It was just coincidence us meeting up again like this.'

Bannock shook his head. 'You've got me wrong, Bat,' the marshal parried, raising his hands. 'Fact is, my deputy has left. Reckons there's more money to be made with the new silver strike in Colorado. So I was wondering if'n you wanted the job. It pays good. And you get to collect a percentage of all fines.' He cast a questioning glance at the younger man. 'What do you say?'

Bat was stunned into silence. The offer had taken him by surprise. He looked down at Herby Alcock. This was the chance for which he had been seeking. The fact registered on his beaming face.

Herby read his mind. 'If'n that's what you want, Bat, then don't let me stand in your way.'

'You sure you don't mind me bunking off? Who's gonna ride shotgun?'

'Let me worry about that,' said the agent, brushing off Bat's concerns. 'If'n it comes to the worst I'll do the job myself.'

In a single bound Bat jumped to the ground and grabbed hold of the marshal's iron hand. 'Looks like you've got yourself a new deputy, Sam.'

Steel-eye clapped his new assistant on the back as they turned and strode back towards the jailhouse. Bat couldn't wait to be sworn in and pin on the revered tin star of a US deputy marshal.

'The main part of this job is managing the cowboys who flood in here at the end of the summer drives,' Bannock informed his new deputy.

Abilene was the first of the true cattle towns that were developing solely for the purpose of shipping cattle back East. Joseph McCoy had recognized its potential and had built holding pens beside the railroad. Known as the 'City of the Plains', Abilene grew rapidly after 1867 primarily due to the trade in beef on the hoof.

Steel-eye Sam peered out of the office window. 'Don't be fooled by the town's sleepy image during the day,' he commented while pouring coffee into a mug. 'It comes alive after dark when the cowpokes arrive. Those fellas can get mighty wild after three months on the trail. Most are just out for a good time. They often spend all the dough they've accrued in a week, before drifting back down to Texas just to do it all over again.'

'What about the others?' enquired Bat, noting the louring frown on his boss's rugged face.

'Those are the ones you have to look out for,' murmured the pensive lawman. 'Too much hard liquor and they can turn real nasty. You have to stamp on them hard before anyone gets killed. Only problem is, you never can tell until the shooting starts. Then it can be too late. The knack is spotting the troublemakers and keeping them under observation. Only after acquiring that skill can you call yourself a real peace officer.'

'So what's my first job?' asked Bat, eager to get started.

Bannock handed him a pile of forms. 'Paperwork,' he grumbled. 'The bane of the job. Everything has to be reported and filed. Might as well get used to it. It ain't all rip-roaring shoot-'em-ups if'n that's what you figured. Go get the details of those two critters back there.' He jerked a thumb towards the cellblock. 'After that you can mosey on down to Maggy May's Diner and get their breakfast. Nothing too tasty, mind,' he added with a grin.

The marshal settled himself in his favourite chair and planted his boots up on the desk too. He emitted a satisfied sigh of contentment. 'Work hard and you'll soon get to be a full marshal. Unlike that lazy critter who just left.' The marshal leaned back, hands behind his head. 'Yes sirree. Old Sam Bannock's gonna enjoy having you around.'

Bat couldn't help but laugh. He didn't mind at all. If'n you wanted something, best to start at the bottom and work your way up.

For the next six months, Bat learned every aspect of the lawman's trade. He became a vital and effective support for Steel-eye Sam Bannock.

The crunch came one day when Bat was out of town investigating the whereabouts of some stolen horses. It turned out to be a wild-goose chase. On his arrival back in Abilene a shock awaited him.

The marshal had been shot in the back by a bushwhacker hiding on a roof.

Bat immediately went after the killer.

He caught up with the skunk in Salina, which was the next town west along the railroad.

A gunfight ensued when Three-gun Charley Picket refused to surrender his weapons. During the contretemps, Bat learned that Picket had been harbouring a grudge against the old lawman after Bannock killed his brother.

He left Charley Picket on the street in a pool of blood. Curious dogs sniffed at the coppery scent while passers-by gave the gruesome heap a wide berth. After reporting the incident to the local undertaker, Bat returned to Abilene, where another surprise awaited him.

During his absence the town council had unanimously agreed to his election as a full-time marshal with all the benefits accruing to that position.

Bat readily accepted.

For the next six months he carried out his duties

with diligence and fairness. Justice was dispensed with neither fear nor favour. Then another noteworthy incident occurred out of the blue.

It was a Saturday night. The town was buzzing as usual.

Bat was patrolling the eastern end of town when a series of shots rang out cutting through the fetid atmosphere. Nothing unusual in that. Abilene was used to cowboys blasting off into the air. It was just part of their normal way of letting off steam.

But this was different.

A panic-stricken voice echoed down the street. It was Ellie Simmonds, who owned the Cattle Queen saloon, which was the largest in town. Ellie operated a well-run establishment which rarely saw any serious trouble. Something bad must have occurred to bring her out in this state of fright.

'Marshal! Marshal! Come quick!' she hollered lifting her voluminous skirts high as she ran towards the surprised lawman. Her normally well-brushed locks were in disarray as she stumbled to a halt. Bat just managed to catch the woman before she tripped up in the dust.

'Hold on there, Ellie,' he soothed, helping the saloon owner to gather herself together. 'What in thunder has gotten you so all het up like this.'

Ellie sucked in a deep lungful of air, ample bosom heaving as she blurted out what had happened. Her waving arm pointed back the way she had come.

'Wagtail Watkins has been shot.'

Watkins was the head bartender at the Queen. As

soon as he heard this, Bat drew his gun and checked the load. Turning about he led the woman by the arm back up the street.

'Some guy wouldn't take no for an answer when Wagtail refused to extend his credit.' She stooped for a moment to get her breath back, panting hard before continuing: 'Then he started shooting at the glasses lined up behind the bar. The mirror exploded in a million pieces. If'n he ain't stopped, someone is going to get killed.' The distraught woman shook her head. 'Ain't seen nothing like this since Pete Macgraw shot the banjo player last fall for playing a tune he didn't like.'

Bat didn't need to ask anything more. Two minutes later they reached the swing doors of the saloon. 'You wait out here while I deal with this varmint.' Ellie huffed some, wanting to join him. 'No, Ellie. Stay out here. This jasper is dangerous, and defusing situations like this is what I'm paid for.' His tone was adamant and Ellie acceded.

Without further ado the lawman pushed through the doors and into the saloon. All the patrons had scurried to the far corners of the room and were hiding under upturned tables and behind anything else that offered protection from flying bullets. Wagtail Watkins was trying to staunch a badly bleeding shoulder with a bar towel.

Leaning on the bar was a heavyset jasper, dressed in grubby range gear. Bat's keen sense of smell picked up the acrid stench of three months' accumulated sweat mixed with stale liquor. The guy had a pistol in each hand and was waving them both around.

One suddenly blasted and an expensive chandelier specially imported from Chicago exploded in a myriad of tiny pieces. Outside, Ellie cried out aloud. That had been her pride and joy.

More important, however, for Bat Madison was the fact that he recognized the gunslinging cowboy. It was none other than his old sidekick, Pike Roswell.

The ex-Ruffian had not seen him enter the saloon, so intent was he on potshotting at the chandelier. Bat crept up behind him, stopping some six feet away. He coughed, a deliberate noise to attract the other man's attention.

Roswell swayed on his boot heels and spun round, clutching at the bar rail. He was clearly the worse for wear. Bleary eyes peered at the newcomer. Struggling to focus them, he leaned forward. A puzzled frown indicated that the face staring at him was somehow familiar.

He prodded a gun at the lawman.

'Do I know you, mister?' he drawled, slurring his words.

Bat ignored the question. 'Hand over those guns, Pike. The party's over.'

Roswell lurched back a pace and laughed.

'Waaal,' he drawled. 'If'n it ain't my old partner, Bearclaw Madison.' Then a bleary eye fastened on to the glinting tin star. 'Seems like you got your wish in the end, old buddy.' An evil gleam appeared in the soused guy's frosty peepers. 'Now you're gonna have to earn your keep. I allus wondered which of us was the faster draw. Time to find out.'

Roswell dropped his guns back into their holsters and settled into the exaggerated posture assumed by gunfighters. Bat suppressed a laugh. It was like one of those music-hall farces that often visited the frontier towns, except that in this instance the stooge was deadly serious.

'Go for your gun,' Roswell slurred as he struggled to remain upright. 'I'll count to three, then we draw.' He belched loudly before hiccuping. 'One . . . two. . . .'

Before Roswell could utter the final count, Bat hooked out his own gun. Quickly he stepped forward and slammed it down on Roswell's head. The drunk uttered a low groan and slumped to the floor. He was out cold. More on account of the liquor he had imbibed than the cushioned blow to the head, his hat having absorbed much of the impact.

'Some of you boys get this critter over to the jailhouse,' Bat ordered, replacing his six shooter in its holster. 'And you best inform the trail boss that he will be one man down when you leave town.'

Next morning Roswell, after he had sobered up, was fully expecting to be released from custody. The most he expected following the previous night's hell-raising was perhaps a fine and a friendly talk over breakfast about keeping on the straight and narrow.

He was to be sadly disillusioned.

Bat considered Roswell's actions to be deadly serious; he had no intentions of showing any

86

favouritism towards past associates. Loyalty to his old partner was a thing of the past. It was history, and meant nothing where the breaking of the law was concerned.

Pike Roswell would face due process before the circuit judge.

'Judas!' the felon spat out from behind the cell bars when he realized there would be no leniency shown. 'Doesn't our riding together with the Ruffians mean anything to you?'

'Last night you nearly killed a man, and shot up the premises of a good friend of mine. If'n you was figuring that could be overlooked, then you're a durned fool. There's nothing more to be said on the matter.'

With that the marshal left the cell block, but with a stark warning ringing in his ears.

'You ain't heard the last of this, Madison,' growled the irate prisoner. 'Pike Roswell looks out for his friends. But he also hunts down his enemies. You better watch out, mister. Because I'll come looking for you. And next time it'll be a sober man that calls you out.'

In the event Roswell received six months hard labour on a chain gang. If anything could sour his opinion of the guy who put him there, then slaving from dawn 'til dusk with a bullwhip tickling your spine was surely it.

Bat Madison also knew that his days in Abilene were numbered. Whether or not Pike Roswell was the faster with a handgun was immaterial. He had no wish to find out, having a new wife to consider.

Three months later, he resigned as marshal of Abilene. A wagon and team were purchased and the young couple headed West in the company of a wagon train. There would be plenty of other towns willing to hire an experienced law officer.

Time passed. Bearclaw Madison forgot about his old partner and the wild threat of revenge he had promised.

Until now.

NINE

NO STAGE FOR ALBUQUERQUE

Bat was given no further time to cogitate on his past association with Pike Roswell.

An approaching swirl of dust caught his attention. It was coming from the west. Could it be the late stage? Or were those danged Indians making another attack on the relay station?

The ex-lawman stubbed out his cigar and screwed up his eyes trying to probe the eddying yellow curtain. The vague form of a single horse appeared at the edge of the corral. A man was in the saddle, a white man. The animal stumbled to a halt. The man teetered then slid over crashing to the ground.

'Man injured!' Bat's urgent warning was accompanied by his fist hammering on the closed door of the station. 'Grab your guns and get out here fast!'

Not waiting for a response, he dashed across the open yard towards the fallen rider. His own weapon palmed, Bat scanned the immediate vicinity for any signs of an imminent attack. Nothing moved to disturb the macabre quietude of the setting.

The man had not moved since falling off his horse.

Bat dropped to his knees and gently cradled the bleeding form in his arms. He unfastened the tight collar around the man's neck, allowing him to breathe more easily. An eye flickered. At least he *was* still breathing.

'It's all right, fella.' Bat hushed the badly wounded man. 'You're safe now. So don't try to speak.'

The man opened his mouth, ignoring the request. A suprisingly strong grip fastened on to Bat's arm. 'It was the . . . Navajo. . .' The grating croak emerged barely above a whisper. 'Bandits tried to rob the stage . . . shot the driver and guard . . . horses stampeded. . . .'

His strength rapidly fading, the man slumped back. Recognizing the guy from their failed robbery, Roswell drew back, furtively urging his partners to do the same. The last thing needed now was to have the finger of guilt pointed his way.

'Let me see to him,' said Maisie Kingman pushing through the hovering bystanders. 'Give the guy some room, can't you?'

The manager's wife bent down to check on the man's injuries. A brief examination was enough for her to know that he was done for. She looked up at her husband. A brisk shake of the head said it all.

But Maisie had a warm and generous heart. Attempting to offer the dying man some hope, she said, 'Ain't nothing but a scratch, mister. We'll soon have you fixed up good as new.'

Jacob Lander was not fooled. The whiskey drummer forced a weak smile.

'Appreciate your . . . concern, sister, but I know . . . different,' he gasped, coughing up a spume of blood. 'No man could survive . . . two bullet wounds . . . and a war lance in his back.'

Bat also knew that the guy didn't have more than a few moments left. He was waning fast. The ex-lawman wanted to learn the full story before the final round-up.

'What happened to the coach?' he asked.

Bleary eyes, bloodshot and blank, tried focusing on the speaker. Ragged bleats rasped in his dry throat. Maisie dribbled water on to the blistered lips. It seemed to rally him. He smiled his thanks.

'After the bandits left empty-handed, the Indians attacked us . . . I was the only survivor. I managed to crawl away . . . behind some rocks.' A haunted look came into his fading eyes. 'Had to watch the others . . . having their hair lifted.' Lander's head drooped. His eyes closed.

Bat shook him. 'The coach,' he urged in a less than tender manner. 'What happened to it?'

Kingman drew him aside. The rather brusque treatment of the injured man did not sit well. 'Easy there, Bat,' he admonished his guest. 'There's no call

91

for any rough handling. The guy's hurt bad. You pushing him around won't make things any clearer.'

Bat recognized that the manager was right. He instantly regretted his impatience. 'Sorry about that. Guess I'm a mite anxious to get Miss Newbold back to Albuquerque after all the hurt she's suffered at the hands of these varmints.' Reining back his impatience, he turned a more sympathetic eye towards Jacob Lander.

Wearily, the injured man forced himself up on to one elbow. 'The redskins . . . the coach. . . .' He grated the words harshly as more frothy blood bubbled up. The ghastly noise sounded like a death rattle. Everybody hung on what they expected to be Lander's final utterance. 'They . . . burned it.'

Still Madison persisted though he knew the guy was finished. Every bit of information that could be squeezed from the dying man was vital.

'Did you hear anything about. . . .' He paused, looking up at the drawn features of Eleanor Newbold. 'About a woman kidnapped by the Navajo?'

Once again the drummer appeared to rally. He gave a fatigued nod and forced out his last words.

'Reward offered . . . for her . . . rescue . . . has been. . . .' The gaps between the laboured utterances were getting longer. Only seconds remained. The listeners strained to hear the weak voice, each man hanging on every laboured syllable. 'Has been . . . raised to . . . twenty. . . .'

A sigh like a deflating balloon issued from

between the bloodless lips. Jacob Lander had breathed his last.

After closing the wildly staring eyes Bat slowly rose to his feet along with Maisie Kingman. Behind them, Roswell gave a wry smile, aiming a wink at his two buddies. He nudged Frank Craddock in the ribs, his eyes lighting up in malicious glee. A doubling of the original sum. Now more than ever, the outlaw intended sticking to his old partner like a bee to a honeypot.

They were in the clear. Now that the last passenger of the unlucky stagecoach was dead, there was nothing to connect them to the incident.

So pleased was Roswell at the outcome that he offered to lay the dead man to rest. 'Me and the boys will see that he gets buried proper,' Roswell intoned in a suitably dolorous voice.

'That's mighty decent of you, Mr Roswell,' Maisie Kingman replied. 'It's good to know there are still plenty of clean-living men in the West.'

Roswell bowed, offering his most sincere smile. The other two outlaws followed suit. Only Bat Madison knew how shallow those unctuous smiles truly were. He sidled up to the gang leader laying a hand on the outlaw's arm and drawing him to a halt. The pair faced each other.

'Guess there ain't no point asking if that stage hold-up had anything to do with you?' Bat's enquiry was brusquely delivered.

Roswell leaned back on his boot heels, hands resting on his hips. Mockingly, he shook his head.

'You sure don't think much of me, do you, old buddy? And after all we went through during the war.'

'Just answer the question, Pike. Did you rob that stage?'

Roswell assumed his most persuasive and meaningful stance before answering. 'I can assure you, Bat, that me and the boys had nothing to do with robbing that stagecoach. And that is God's honest truth.' Roswell turned to his two partners for their support. 'Ain't that so, you guys?'

'Sure is,' agreed Frank Craddock. 'Must have been some other outfit that carried out such a bad deed. Sure weren't us.' He had quickly cottoned on to his boss's assertion. It was true. They hadn't pulled off the robbery. The intent had been there, but no reward.

A mite slow on the uptake, Tom was about to spoil the charade when Frank dug him hard in the ribs. His brother winced but quickly got the message to keep a tight lip.

Bat missed the sly manoeuvre. His attention was wholly focused on Roswell and his sly rejection of the charge laid at his door.

The tall Kentuckian was not wholly convinced. But he had no option but to accept Pike Roswell's denial of any involvement. He offered it a brisk grunt before moving away.

There were other matters that now required his consideration.

Bat was fully cognizant of the problem with which

he had been saddled, and could well have done without. Namely, being left with the woman on his hands. Much as he had been attracted to Eleanor Newbold, in truth he knew that the lady was spoken for and out of his reach.

His quest lay elsewhere. Bat Madison's avowed mission to continue the search for his own missing wife was no less important to him.

So where did that leave him now?

He would have to accompany the lady back to Albuquerque. The increased reward did not figure in his decision. Contrary to Pike Roswell's insinuations, his was a duty of care and responsibility. Opting out was unthinkable.

The next morning dawned fine and bright. Bat was saddling his horse out in the barn when Pike Roswell sidled up behind him.

'Me and the boys have been talking,' he said casting a languid eye on his old partner's back. 'We figure that with all these redskins about, you're gonna need some extra help in escorting Miss Newbold back to Albuquerque.'

It was a statement of intent. Roswell had made up his mind.

Bat's jawed tightened. Slowly he turned to face the smirking outlaw.

'Don't suppose that the reward has anything to do with this sudden change in your plans, has it?'

Roswell shrugged. 'Just doing my bounden duty as a good citizen, is all.' The look hardened to one of stony determination. 'You got a beef agin that?'

This time it was Bat's turn to raise a listless shoulder. 'You do as you please. But don't think for one minute about trying to get rid of me along the trail. I'll be watching you and your buddies like a hawk.'

Roswell raised a placatory arm. 'Now would I do that to an old buddy? You got me all wrong, Bat. All I want to do is help a lady in distress. And I ain't never visited Albuquerque.' Then he spun on his heel and walked away. 'Besides,' he threw back over his shoulder. 'It's a five-day ride. Anything could happen along the way.'

The ominous threat hung in the still air like the sword of Damocles.

Bat's expression hardened. He needed Roswell and his gang to fight off any Indian attack. But he could not watch the varmints all the time. Everybody had to sleep at some point. That would be when he was at his most vulnerable.

He continued loading the mule with supplies for the five-day trek, tossing over the implications in his mind.

A half-hour later the unlikely group of riders was ready to leave. Maisie Kingman had prepared some vittles which she handed to Bat. 'There's a few tasty treats in there to brighten up your trail grub. Don't go eating them all at once, you hear?'

Bat gave a brisk salute. 'No ma'am,' he breezed, aiming a wry smirk at a slavering Pike Roswell. He recalled how his old partner had a sweet tooth. 'I'll make sure they're rationed out fairly.'

He then shook hands with the station manager. 'Good luck to you, Bat,' Kingman declared in a mournful voice. 'I reckon you're gonna need it.'

Once again Bat's face assumed an expression of firm resolve. 'I'll get through,' he averred forcefully. 'No Navajo are gonna feel my hair, nor that of Miss Newbold.' No mention was made of his other companions. They could take their chances.

TEN

IN DEEP

The small procession moved off at a gentle trot.

For the next hour they followed the well-rutted trail used by the overland stage and mule trains bound for Prescott to the south-west. A prominent landmark known as the Ganado Needle marked a distinct swing of the trail to the north-east and Farmington.

Following this would add a further three days to their journey. Although it was the safer option, Bat was not prepared to sacrifice the time-saving. In addition, he figured that by heading due east they would avoid an undesirable meeting with Shongopovi and his skittish bucks.

The new route was barely more than a deer run. Twisting and looping through the broken mesa country, it was difficult to see further than the next rocky hillock. Around noon they took a rest for coffee and some of those treats provided by Maisie Kingman.

'You know where we're headed?' enquired a sceptical Pike Roswell biting into a sugar-coated doughnut. 'Seems to me like we'd have made better time sticking to the main trail.'

They were camped in a rocky arroyo carved out by the unpredictable flash floods that had their origins in the distant Chuska Mountains. Although infrequent, they could make a devastating impact on those caught in their violent path. A clear sky could be a deceptive illusion.

'I know exactly what I'm doing,' stressed Bat, casting a bleak eye towards the gathering cloud banks to the north. 'If'n you don't like it, the answer is simple.' He threw a challenging look towards the gang boss. 'You and your buddies can always pull out.'

'Just thinking aloud, is all,' countered Roswell with a shrug. He wiped the sticky sugar from his mouth. 'We'll tag along. Just to make sure the dame gets home in one piece.'

The lady in question was over on the far side of the gully tidying herself up. Tom Craddock was feeding the horses while his brother stood guard on a bluff overlooking the campsite.

Seeing that Eleanor Newbold was out of earshot, Roswell spat out a warning in a lowered voice that was intended for Bat's ears only.

'Don't be thinking you can get rid us that easily. I aim to cut me a wad of that reward. In fact, I might well take the whole caboodle.'

Bat growled out a furious retort. His body tensed, the craggy face became flushing with indignation. He jumped to his feet, fists bunching, ready to beat the hell out of this unwanted reminder of his past. 'I've just about had enough of your—'

He never got to complete the threatened beating. A sharp call from Frank Craddock effectually smothered the brewing confrontation.

'Hey, Pike!' he shouted down to the others. 'I reckon them Indians can't be far away.'

The clash between the two old partners was pushed aside for the present. 'Can you see them?' Pike shouted back.

'No, but I can see their smoke,' Frank replied, pointing towards a distant ridge that was unseen by those below. 'There must be two bands signalling to one another. And they can't be more than three or four miles away.'

'Time we was on the move,' snapped Bat, pouring the dregs of the coffee over the fire.

Within minutes they were mounted up and galloping full pelt along the arroyo. The last place Bat wanted to be caught was in such a position where they could be picked off like rats in a barrel. Better to get out into the open where they could at least see their enemy.

The ominous rumble of thunder over the Chuskas appeared to bode ill for the small party.

They rode hard for the next hour. But the horses could not maintain such a furious pace for long in this heat. Nervous eyes constantly scanned the horizon for any signs of the threatened Indian attack. Thankfully they did not put in an appearance.

Satisfied that they had managed to evade the Indians, Bat slowed to a steady trot. He knew, however, that it was only a temporary reprieve.

All Indians possessed the uncanny knack of being able to blend into their environment. The soaring bluffs and mesas characteristic of desert terrain in this part of Arizona were their home. Furthermore, they were excellent trackers. It was the white man who was the intruder in an alien landscape where survival became an ever-present struggle.

Bat had little doubt that Shongopovi would not be held at bay for long. But he kept this disturbing piece of knowledge under wraps. They were riding along the crest of a ridge on the left hand side of a deep cleft. Some 500 feet below, the tumbling waters of the Chaco Wash had carved out a ravine known as Crystal Gulch.

White horses could been seen in the wild ferment, glinting like jewels in the sunlight. The depth of the ravine carved out by the poweful torrent testified to the powerful force of water. An awesome sight.

On the far side, stands of Douglas fir and ponderosa pine cloaked the steep flanks of the cutting. That was in stark contrast to the stony trail that they were now following, which had narrowed to little more than six feet wide. As a result, the riders were forced into single file.

To their left rose a vertical upthrust of bare rock.

Small stones tumbling from the heights above were a constant hazard. The possibility of large boulders crashing down on to them posed a dangerous threat. On the other side, the narrow trail plunged abruptly down into the gulch.

Frank Craddock was in the lead with Bat close behind. To his rear was Roswell, with the other two following him.

'Keep into the cliff face,' Bat shouted over his shoulder. 'One slip here and we're done for.'

They edged gingerly along the cramped ledge. Tom Craddock at the back, clutching hold of the mule rope; fear was etched on his face. He had always suffered from a dread of heights.

Roswell's eyes burned with a fiercely exhilarating intensity. This was his chance to get rid of Madison once and for all.

Drawing a deep breath into his lungs, the outlaw jabbed the sharp spur rowels viciously into the flanks on his mount. The cayuse neighed. It instinctuvely jumped forward, crashing into the rear of Bat's own horse. The shocked animal reared up in fright. Its hoofs were slipping on the loose gravel. Bat felt himself being pushed towards the deadly rim of the downfall.

Desperately he struggled to control the panicking horse.

It was Frank Craddock who saved him from certain death. The elder brother immediately read the signs. Reaching behind, he grabbed hold of the paint's bridle and forced its bobbing head away from the edge of the ravine. This vital action alone was sufficient to turn the skittish mare away from imminent danger.

Bat exhaled a deep sigh of relief. 'Much obliged to you, Frank,' he gasped, knowing that his life had been in the balance. 'You surely saved me from the Grim Reaper's clutches.'

The elder Craddock merely smiled an acknowledgement.

Roswell couldn't hide a withering scowl. But he instantly transformed the snarl into a look of abject contrition before anybody noticed.

'Gee, Bat,' he warbled, 'I sure am sorry about that. This danged nag slipped and my spurs must have panicked him.'

Bat responded with a sour grimace. He suspected the truth. The main thing now was to reach the end of this ledge safe and sound. They continued onward for another fifteen minutes before the trail widened.

Following the traumatic ordeal of crossing the narrow ledge, Bat called a halt. They all needed to rest with some coffee and vittles. During the brief halt, Roswell once again protested his innocence of any skulduggery. Bat shrugged him off. He didn't believe the guy's weasel words for a minute. But there was no proof of any foul play. To all intents and purposes, it was a pure accident.

Thereafter, however, the two ex-Border Ruffians kept their distance.

While Bat was catching his breath he once again voiced his appreciation of Frank Craddock's swift action. His shaking hands nursed a welcome mug of strong coffee as he regarded the younger man curiously before venturing a more personal query.

'I hope you don't mind me saying this, Frank,' he iterated with a measure of hesitation, 'but you don't seem the type of guy who would normally hang out with someone like Pike Roswell.'

Craddock gave the strange remark a quizzical frown. 'What are you getting at, Mr Madison?'

'I suppose he's told you already that we rode together during the war.' Bat took a moment to build a couple of stogies. He passed one to Frank, scratched a vesta on a rock and lit them both. Frank nodded his thanks, waiting for the other man to continue. 'What he might not have mentioned is that I was instrumental in getting him convicted and sentenced to serve time on a Kansas chain gang.'

Frank thought for minute. 'No, you're right, he never mentioned that. Not that I would hold it against him. Me and Tom ain't exactly blue-eyed angels ourselves.'

'What I'm trying to say, Frank, is that a smart young fella like you could make something a heap better for himself.'

'And what about Tom?' asked Craddock pointedly. 'If'n I was to branch out on my ownsome, he'd be lost. Like as not get himself in deep trouble. I couldn't let that happen. Not to my own brother. I owe it to our ma to see that Tom's taken care of.'

Frank Craddock paused for a moment to reflect on the circumstances of his life. 'Our pa was an evil bastard.' The harsh invective came as a shock to Bat, so venomous was its ferocity. 'He used to beat us for no good reason. We both had to endure it. But then I grew up. The hard graft on the farm made me lean and muscular. One time he pushed me too far. And I hit back. A mite too hard as it happened, if'n you catch my drift?'

Bat nodded. He understood.

'I couldn't stick around after that. So me and Tom lit out on our own. I send money back for Ma as often as I can. But I ain't seen her for nigh on a year. It's difficult going back to Missouri, knowing there's still a warrant out for me.'

Both men sat smoking in silence for a few minutes, each one digesting the import of these revelations.

Frank was the first to break the reflective mood.

'Pike has been good to us,' he said in support of his leader. 'Offered to take us on at a time when we needed it. And he always splits any dough we make three ways. Unlike some other jaspers that we've ridden with who keep the lion's share for themselves.'

This was not what Bat wanted to hear. 'Well, if'n you need any help to take a different course, let me know,' he offered. He stood up. Then he called out to the others. 'Time to hit the trail, folks.'

They hadn't been riding for more than ten minutes when the easy silence was shattered by a full-throated series of whoops. Bat's worst fears had been realized. Even though he'd tried to conceal their movements from the Indians, Shongopovi's tracking ability was second to none. The Navajo chief had managed to pick up their trail, seemingly with effortless ease.

Leathers slapping, the five riders urged their mounts to a frenetic gallop. For ten minutes they succeeded in keeping the Indians at a distance.

At some point during the headlong dash along the rim of Crystal Gulch they had crossed over the territorial border into New Mexico. Nobody was aware of this political divide, least of all the pursuing Indians.

Suddenly, with Bat in the lead, the fugitives reached a distinct break in the flat mesa. A tributary creek had been carved out over millennia into a deep rift which blocked their onward progress.

Bat veered left along the edge of the downfall, searching desperately for a safe means to descend into the yawning chasm below.

He was in luck.

The branch canyon was shallow, falling away at its extremity in a scree slope. It would entail much sliding and deft control of their horses to prevent any falls. But there was no other choice open to them.

'Head on down into the gorge,' he shouted, swinging the paint down through the tree cover. 'On the far bank of Chaco Wash we'll stand a better chance of holding them off.'

It was fortunate indeed that the gradient had eased noticeably. The horses slithered and fumbled their way down the bank of loose stones. It required all their riders' concentrated effort to remain in the saddles. At the bottom of ravine they came out of the trees on to a flat shelf of rock. It lay thirty feet above the waters of the wash.

There was no option but to force the horses to leap over the edge into the waters below. Fortunately, at this point the fractured rocks of the gorge had been weakened over time, enabling the water to erode the sides much faster. Less constricted, the churning ferment of the wash had broadened out into a more gently flowing lake within an amphitheatre of rocky walls.

Roswell was the first to reach the far shore. The others quickly followed. Only Tom Craddock was lagging behind as he struggled with the pack mule.

'Come on, little brother!' hollered Frank, urging his younger sibling onwards. 'You can make it.' The concern in Frank Craddock's voice was clearly audible to the others as they watched the kid's leaden exertions. Frank was only too well aware that his brother could not swim.

Suddenly the mule panicked. It jerked the rope that Tom was holding and dragged him off the horse into the deep water. Tom screamed, throwing up his arms in dismay. The fearful yell was cut short as he disappeared from view, swallowed up by the deep waters of the lake.

It was only for a second. His head bobbed up. But it was clear to the gaping watchers that he could not survive unaided.

'Someone save him!' shrieked Frank, standing on the edge of the wash. All his natural reserve was discarded in the face of this awful scenario. For Frank

Craddock was also a non-swimmer. The impotence that he felt was conveyed to the others, who exhorted the flailing Coyote Kid to grab hold of one of the animals.

But the mule was already being swept away by the current. The horse was also out of reach as it thrashed towards the safety of the bank. Tom Craddock was on his own. Roswell stood back. No way was he putting his own life at risk. Unlike the others, whose attention was wholly focused on the drowning kid, he had spotted the Indians on the rim high above the gorge.

Already they were edging down the scree run. In minutes they would be on the narrow ledge over-looking the lake.

The responsibility to do something was left squarely in Bat's hands.

He didn't hesitate.

The kid was tiring fast. Another minute and he would go under and not return to the surface. Bat shucked off his gunbelt, boots and hat and splashed into the shallows before diving into the rapidly deepening wash. Strong powerful strokes cut a swath through the rippling waters. The kid was only twenty yards out, but under such circumstances it seemed like a mile.

'It's OK, Tom,' he shouted between heaving breaths. 'Hang in there. I'll not let you drown.'

Seconds later his powerful arms gripped the thrashing kid, his voice urging him to quieten down. 'You ain't doing either of us any favours by struggling,' he stressed firmly.

After turning Craddock on to his back, Bat placed an arm around his chest so that the kid's head was lifted clear of the water. Then he started on the arduous return to the near bank. Shouts of exhortation urged him on to maximum effort: an effort all the more vital when he heard Roswell's warning that the Indians were dismounting on the far shore.

The muted sound of gunfire penetrated his fuzzy brain. His muscles ached like the devil and felt like they were on fire. How much further to the bank? He struggled onward. Then his feet touched bottom. He gave a sigh of relief. Scrambling up the sloping gravel, he dragged the kid's inert body out of the water.

'You're . . . safe now . . . Tom,' he panted, struggling to draw breath into tortured lungs. But there was no response.

The Coyote Kid was a dead weight. An arrow protruded from his chest. There was no way of knowing how long it had been there.

Frank rushed across. He grabbed his brother and dragged the bleeding corpse behind the protection of a boulder. Roswell and the woman offered covering fire as more arrows zipped all around.

The elder Craddock stroked his kid brother's waxy face, murmuring pleas for him to come round. But there was no response.

It was left for Eleanor to gently prise the two Craddocks apart. She held Frank like a baby, cooing and whispering gentle nothings to soothe his anguish.

'He's gone to a better place, Frank,' she said at length.

Beside her, Pike Roswell was more concerned with the living, particularly the safety of his own skin. Frantically working the lever action of his Winchester, he continued pumping shells at the whooping Indians.

Suddenly the frenetic cheering ceased.

Shongopovi stepped forward and stood on the edge of the shelf above the lake. Displaying a disdainful contempt, he arrogantly defied the lethal barrage of shots. The Navajo chief's arms were raised in thanksgiving as he cried out gratitude to the Great Spirit for delivering the defiler of his daughter. The plagent cadences were intended to strike fear into the hearts of those who remained alive.

Bullets zipped around the swaying chief. But none found its mark.

Still floundering in the shallows, Bat Madison alone was unaffected by the the tormenting spectacle. The stark truth that he had saved a dead man was a stunning blow. Bullets whistled around his head. But he was totally unaware that they originated from his own Winchester.

It was Roswell's harsh bark that eventually urged him to seek shelter.

'Get off your damned ass,' roared the gang boss, 'if'n you don't want a dose of the same.'

Even as he bellowed out the warning, Roswell regretted the outburst. His jaw tightened in self-reproach. If he had left the guy the Navajo would have finished him off, leaving Pike free to collect the reward money with no risk of any charges hanging over him.

Too late now. The warning had been a reflex action to save his old comrade from the threat of certain death. Old loyalties died hard. A pity that Madison hadn't felt the same back in Abilene.

Bat nodded his thanks as he scrambled to safety. He received nought but a curt grunt in response.

Then, as abruptly as it had begun, the haunting thanksgiving from Shongopovi stopped. The Indians disappeared like a dream in the night.

ELEVEN

ACCIDENTAL ENCOUNTER

Bat fingered the bearclaw necklace. The potent talisman had always helped him in the past. Now it succeeded in bringing him to his senses, dispelling the lethargy that had threatened to overwhelm him. A dark cloud was lifted from his fuzzy brain.

Imbued with a renewed vigour, he ordered Frank Craddock to ride downstream. His aim was to determine whether there was an easy crossing of Chaco Wash that the Indians might use.

'Hasn't Frank suffered enough already?' the woman protested. 'His brother has just been killed.'

'I know that. But this ain't no time for shilly-shallying,' Madison shot back impatiently. 'Sure, I'm sorry about Tom catching it. But we have to think

112

about ourselves now. And we don't need a heap of soft-soaping at a time like this.'

Eleanor's face assumed a russet hue of indignation. She was clearly rattled by this man's criticism of her care and concern for another human being. Her whole body tensed as she stood up to have it out with the heartless fiend.

'How dare you speak to me like that,' she railed, hands firmly planted on shapely hips. 'The least you can do is accord him the chance to come to terms with the loss,' she concluded angrily.

'Frank has to pull himself together,' Bat responded forcefully. 'Those Indians might well have been satisfied with getting their revenge. But then again, their blood could be up. Finishing us all off might just be the icing on the cake for Shongopovi. And I don't intend to take any chances.' Having delivered that brusque rejoinder he turned his attention once again to addressing the surviving Craddock. 'You ready then, Frank?'

The outlaw now felt shamefaced at having displayed his feelings so openly.

'It's all right, ma'am,' he answered, standing up and squaring his shoulders. 'Mr Madison is right. There's only three of us left to protect you now that Tom's hit the high trail. We can't afford to relax for a minute until you've been delivered safely back to your family in Albuquerque.'

As far as Bat was concerned the matter was now closed.

'We'll make camp here while you're away,' he said

from between teeth that had suddenly begun to chatter.

Bat's clothes were saturated, making him shiver violently from the cold. The sun had now dropped below the western horizon taking all its heat with it. Quickly he began to gather up driftwood to build a fire.

'It'll be dark inside of two hours. That ought to give you enough light to suss out the lie of the land downstream aways,' Bat added as Frank Craddock made to spur off along the bank of the creek.

Roswell had been enjoying the vigorous exchange while he sat cleaning his rifle. He couldn't have engineered it better himself. Anything to cause a rift between Bat and Eleanor would considerably assist his plans.

'You shouldn't speak to a lady in that manner,' he said to his old sidekick. 'She was only trying to help the poor sap.'

Pike was pleased to see the woman nodding vigorously in agreement.

Madison ignored the gratuitous comment. 'You two would be better engaged in preparing the evening meal,' he rapped. His whole attention then focused upon cajoling the tinder to catch light.

Bat called for an early start the following morning. Due to the Indian attack and its aftermath, which included Tom Craddock's burial, another day had been lost. He therefore set a fast pace to try to make up the lost time. Luckily they soon passed beyond the meandering constriction of Crystal Gulch, emerging on to an undulating plain of sagebrush and cactus.

Around mid-morning an eagle-eyed Frank Craddock spotted a lone horse in the distance. He pointed to a mottled grey stallion chewing on some gramma grass.

'What in blue blazes is a cayuse doing out here?'

Roswell had voiced the question on everyone's lips. It posed the further question of where its owner could be. As they drew closer it became increasingly clear that the animal was an Indian horse. The fancy blanket and the lack of a saddle were a dead give-way.

Bat signalled a halt. Nervously they all peered around, searching for the other Indians, who ought to be close by. But there was no one else in sight. Neither was there sufficient cover to conceal their presence. Such was the advantage of riding across open terrain.

Where there was a horse, it followed there had to be a rider close by. Guns drawn in case of a surprise attack, they gingerly approached the grey.

Once again it was Frank who was the first to see something. A figure was lying face down behind a clump of beavertail cacti. He leapt off his horse and hustled across to the still form. The long black hair and lithe shape beneath the deerskin attire indicated an Indian girl.

He turned her over. Blood dribbled from a bad cut on her forehead.

'She can't have been here long,' Frank observed. He untied his bandanna and gently dabbed at the wound. 'The blood is still fresh. And it looks like she's broken her leg. The nag must have thrown her. I wonder what caused it to do that?'

His question received a blood-curdling response.

The spine-tingling rattle from the desert's most feared predator sounded in the still air. A large diamondback reared up behind Frank. The snake writhed and swayed, its flat head and staring eyes glaring at this unwelcome interloper. Its forked tongue probed the air as it prepared to strike.

Bat Madison reacted with lightning speed.

He grabbed for his Colt and dispatched three bullets at the lunging serpent. One at least found its target as the ugly head disintegrated in a spattering of bone and sinew. The headless body continued to twitch for a few moments before settling on to the parched ground.

The chilling incident had numbed them all.

'Who is she, do you think?' enquired Eleanor Newbold once she had recovered her composure. But it was her next comment that sparked more of a reaction from the others. 'And I wonder if her tribe are near by.'

'Well, if'n they are,' opined Bat, slotting fresh cartridges into the revolver, 'those shots will bring them running.' His next order was to Roswell. 'You get up on that knoll and see if'n you can see anything.'

Roswell voiced no objections to being ordered around. Like the others he had no wish to encounter Shongopovi again in a hurry.

'Now we know why the horse shied,' remarked

Frank, leaving Eleanor to see to the Indian girl, who was slowly regaining consciousness.

It was a further fifteen minutes before she was able to take in her surroundings. Observing three white faces looming over her brought a terrified set to her beauteous features. She shrank away, assuming it was they who had caused her fall.

'It's all right, my dear,' Eleanor soothed while tying a bandage around the girl's head. 'A snake frightened your horse.' She pointed to the reptile's loathsome remains. 'But you're OK now. We mean you no harm.'

The white woman's mollifying tone seemed to have the desired effect. The girl's satin-smooth features became more serene. Sitting up she accepted a water bottle and proceeded to drain the tepid contents in a single draught.

'What's your name, girl?' asked Bat, using sign language when she had fully regained her senses.

'I am Little White Dove, daughter of the great Navajo chief Shongopovi,' she replied in the white man's tongue. She spoke in a stilted, rather formal manner, learned from her father.

'And what is Little White Dove doing alone in the Socorro desert?' He handed her one of the remaining doughnuts which she wolfed down, then accepted another, which went the same way. 'This is no place for anybody to be travelling alone.'

The girl's lithe form stiffened. 'Navajo born for this land. We are taught from rise of first sun to use desert and see it as a friend. I visit cousin in Angel

Canyon. She married to Anasazi, who are at peace with the Navajo.'

She tried to stand, not realizing that her leg was broken. Eleanor had set it, using some wooden splints obtained from a nearby copse of greasewood. A cry of anguish issued from between the girl's sensuous lips as she sank back on to the hard ground.

Only Pike Roswell had seemed unmoved by the Indian girl's alarm and distress.

But on hearing the name of the girl, he caught the strained look aimed at him from the remaining Craddock. A brief shake of Pike's head warned Frank not to reveal that this was the young woman whom his brother had defiled. That sort of knowledge was best left unspoken.

It was Madison who offered the perfect solution. Pike Roswell could not have planned it better himself.

'I will take Little White Dove back to her tribe.'

Bat helped the girl to her feet. He and Craddock lifted her on to the grey stallion. The splinted leg stuck out to one side. 'You two guys accompany Mrs Newbold. Stick to this trail and I'll catch you up at Medicine Gap. It's a deep split in the mesa wall east of here. You should reach it around noon tomorrow.'

'We'll be there, won't we, Pike?' Frank fastened a bleak eye on to his partner.

'Sure we will,' Roswell concurred with forced joviality. 'The coffee will be bubbling and I'll even save you some of them tasty cakes.'

'Watch your step where Shongopovi is concerned,'

Frank stressed. There was genuine concern in his voice. 'Seeing you with his daughter might give him the wrong idea.'

Roswell scowled. *Let's hope it does,* mused the outlaw, although he kept the notion strictly to himself.

'Don't you worry about me,' Bat replied. 'I'll make sure he sees that I ain't packing any hardware.' He handed Frank the Colt Frontier. 'Maybe when he sees that we are helping out his daughter, he'll leave us alone.'

With Eleanor's help Bat moved away to ready himself for the dangerous ride back into Indian territory. Once they were out of earshot, Pike Roswell drew his buddy to one side.

'You ain't going soft on me, are you, Frank?' he challenged jabbing a finger into his associate's chest.

' 'Course I ain't,' Craddock shot back. 'Just being friendly is all.'

'We ain't along on this expedition to be good buddies,' Roswell warned. 'Far from it.'

His tone hardened.

'You just remember that we're in this together as partners. That dame is worth a heap more than we could make robbing stagecoaches. And it's all legal and above board.' A pause followed as he lit up a cigar before mentioning the main obstacle in their path. 'All we have to do is get rid of Madison.'

Again the gang boss cast a fiercely menacing look at his sidekick.

'Make no mistake about it. That varmint would

run us both in if'n he cottoned on to our past . .
shall we say . . . indiscretions. Once a lawman, always
a lawman.'

'Guess you're right, Pike,' Frank agreed nervously.
'I hadn't thought about it that way.'

Roswell pressed home his advantage.

'All that ho-ha about watching his step. Ain't you
worked it out yet? Without him and Tom, we split the
reward money right down the middle. That's ten big
ones apiece. Enough for you to buy that farm of
your'n in Missouri outright. And there'll be plenty
left over to make sure your ma don't have to work
her fingers to the bone ever again.'

His chin jutted forward as he pressed home the
advantages of an even split.

'You think on that for a spell, Frank. Mr Bearclaw
Bat Madison is all that stands between you and a
small fortune to help ease the burden for the woman
that raised you.'

Roswell moved away. A sly glance told him that his
little talk had struck home. Now he could carry out
the rest of his plan. A seed had been planted in the
younger man's brain. Being nurtured, it would see
Frank Craddock unthinkingly backing his hand
when the time came to eliminate Madison.

Once that skunk was out of the way and the
woman returned to her family, it wouldn't take but a
stray bullet to make sure that the entire reward was
resting in his saddle-bags only.

Then it would be *adios* to New Mexico, and *hola* to
old Mexico.

Ten minutes later Madison bid farewell to his associates, reminding them of the rendezvous at Medicine Gap.

He was placing his trust in the younger man to ensure that the wily Roswell did not attempt any sly trickery.

As usual, Pike Roswell was all uctuous charm, behaving as if skulduggery was the last thing on his mind.

'Time for us to hit the trail, ma'am,' he called, injecting a buoyant note of optimism into the request as he adjusted the saddle leathers on his horse.

TWELVE

BAD MEDICINE

It took the rest of the day to find Shongopovi's camp.

The chief rose from his position outside a temporary shelter made from juniper branches and plaited yucca stems. The others had had to make do with sleeping under the open sky.

He had been expecting the return of his daughter the previous day.

'You are late,' he rasped in a gruff tone that sounded more like the bark of a hound than the greeting of a concerned parent. It was clear that he had not noticed the young woman's misshapen leg, which was on the far side of her horse.

But there was no mistaking the man who was accompanying her. The other braves also recognized one of the men against whom they had so recently been in combat. Arrows were notched on to bow strings as searching eyes scanned the terrain for the other white eyes.

Bat raised both his arms to show that he was unarmed.

'I come in peace, Shongopovi,' he declared in a slow drawl. 'Your daughter was injured in a fall when a rattlesnake frightened her horse. As you can see, her leg is broken. We set it with splints. Perhaps your medicine man can make a potion to ease the pain.

'Is what Bearclaw say right, daughter?' enquired the chief.

Little White Dove winced, her face creasing in pain when her brother Tocahatchi lifted her off the grey.

'Snake would have completed its work had not this man helped me,' she confirmed. 'I owe him my life. Maybe this clumsy wooden head could learn something from him,' she berated her sibling. Tocahatchi was none too pleased by the tongue-lashing from a woman. The sour look aimed at Madison could have curdled milk.

Shongopovi's harsh features softened momentarily. He signalled for one of the braves who acted as the tribal healer to tend his daughter's injuries.

'We thank you, Bearclaw, for your help and concern for my daughter.' The braves briskly nodded their approval of Bat's solicitous act. 'This not what we would have expected from white invaders after my daughter's last encounter at the hands of your fellow countryman.'

Bat gave the remark a puzzled frown. 'I do not

understand,' he said. 'Can Shongopovi explain?'

The chief proceeded to enlighten his guest in a dolorous tone. 'The man calling himself Coyote attacked and ravished my daughter. For that he paid the penalty in the waters of Chaco Wash. Dignity and respect have been achieved. So now we can go home. You brave and honourable man, Bearclaw. What can we do for you?'

'I am heading back to join up with my associates at Medicine Gap. But I have no weapon to protect myself.' His eyes strayed to the Winchester leaning against the chief's shelter.

Much as he wanted its return, he could not voice the request outright. That would be an insult. All he could do was hope and pray.

But it was not to be.

Shongopovi handed over a sheathed knife together with a bow and quiver of arrows. He also arranged for one of the braves to accompany Bearclaw to his destination.

'Other Indians in territory will not be so generous if you encounter them. But with Navajo guardian, you will have unhindered passage.' But there was an ulterior motive in the great chief's assumed magnanimity. 'And at Medicine Gap he can collect rare herbs only found growing there.'

The principal medicine man for the tribe always remained at the home camp, but all expeditions included one brave who had some knowledge of how to treat the varied ailments and injuries sustained in such forays. Medicine men and their acolytes always carried a bag of secret concoctions and talismans to ward off evil spirits and bad juju.

Curative herbs were more practical remedies, but many were difficult to obtain and therefore were sparingly applied.

Medicine Gap was a revered location of herbs such as the Indian turnip used to cure headaches, and wild mint that helped to relieve vomiting. More common were the cones from the spruce tree, which eased sore throats. There was also the lyrically named skunk cabbage to relieve asthma. All these and more could be found in Medicine Gap, from which it had clearly acquired its name.

Before the chief could nominate a brave to accompany the white man, Tocahatchi interjected to offer his services.

'Would this not go some way to allowing me to redeem my reputation and standing in the tribe?' he argued softly but with firm assurance.

He peered around at the listening braves, gauging their reaction to his suggestion. A suitably abject expression cloaked the brave's usually confident features. Restrained nods of acquiescence encouraged him to continue.

'And will not the placing of myself at the service of the man who defeated me in combat be sufficient abasement to clear my shame in the eyes of the tribal council?'

He turned to face his father whose decision was final.

'That is indeed a worthy task for you, my son,'

Shongopovi assented, laying a hand on the boy's shoulder. 'Complete it and your dignity and prestige within the tribe will be restored, with no taint on your character.'

Tocahatchi humbled himself with a deep bow. 'You are truly a great chief, Father. And I will seek only to honour your name amongst the many arms of our tribe upon my return.'

The two unlikely companions rode off soon after. No words were spoken as Bat led the way across the undulating landscape of desiccated sagebrush and mesquite. They rode steadily for three hours. The tension between the two old adversaries was palpable. Bat could feel the Indian's glittering eyes boring into his back. He had no wish for the Indian's war lance to do likewise.

The further the afternoon sun progressed across the azure sky the more uneasy he became. Eating away at his brain was the notion that there was more to this journey than the mere acquisition of rare herbs.

He was not wrong in that conjecture.

Tocahatchi had grasped at this opportunity to avenge himself on the man who had brought scorn upon him in the eyes of his comrades. The fact that he had instigated the circumstances of his downfall was now irrelevant to the incensed Indian.

Somewhere along the trail between the Indian camp and Medicine Gap, his chance finally to rid himself of this dishonourable encumbrance would present itself. He would be ready.

This time there would be nobody around to ensure even-handed gallantry thwarted his plans. The Indian sneered. Such notions were reserved for fools. Only by making certain that he had the advantage could success be guaranteed. What purpose could be served by allowing his opponent an equal chance to compete? To his twisted way of thinking, only those who displayed guile and cunning were worthy of status and prestige amongst their fellows.

Once he had dealt with this strutting turkey he would carry on to Medicine Gap and surprise the other white eyes. A leery smirk creased the Indian's warped features. Then the woman would be his by conquest.

Keeping his eyes peeled Tocahatchi waited patiently for the right moment.

The dry, open expanse of the Socorro Desert presented no opportunity to launch a surprise attack, against which any attempt to retaliate would come too late.

Only when they drew close to Whitehorse Butte did the landscape change to present a more broken appearance. Rock pinnacles amidst the boulders at the plateau's eastern extremity provided ideal terrain for an ambush.

The Navajo ensured that he was in the lead, so as to execute what he had in mind. All he needed was to be out of the white dog's line of sight for a moment.

Bat sensed that his unwelcome escort was planning something. But what it was, or how it would be played out, he had no way of knowing. All he could do was stay alert for any sign of chicanery.

It came as the lengthening shadows were falling across the desolate wilderness.

Tocahatchi had slowly pulled ahead. His pace increased gently so as not to alarm his victim. A hundred yards separated them when he suddenly veered right, behind a bank of red sandstone. The Indian was out of sight for no more than a minute. More than enough time to lay a trap.

As Bat came into view, the Indian was ready for him. In the time it might take to shout *Ambush!* three arrows had been notched, aimed and dispatched.

The first lifted Bat's hat. He could feel the brush of the feathering against his scalp. Another buried itself in his horse's neck. The paint reared up in shock. That was what saved Bat's life as the third arrow sank its barbed head into the poor horse's throat.

The stricken animal stumbled on to its knees and pitched forward. Its rider tumbled on to his back in the sand.

Tocahatchi screamed in fury. But he wasn't finished yet. He grabbed his knife from the buckskin sheath around his waist and flung it at the object of his hatred. The gleaming blade plucked at Bat's shirtsleeve. He felt a searing jolt of fire in his left forearm. But the pain barely registered.

A second knife appeared in the Indian's hand as he dived at this white devil who had the luck of the gods on his side. Bat saw the blurred form soaring through the air towards him. He had a split second to respond. He rolled quickly to one side and the knife plunged into the ground inches from his back. Bat continued to roll over and over in the sand until he was able to scramble to his feet.

He whipped out his own knife and hunkered down.

Now he knew what a scurvy snake in the grass the mighty Tocahatchi really was. Only a yellow rat would plan such a cowardly ambush and show his true colour.

As the thought formed in his mind the Indian jumped up. The white man knew that his scorn could not be read in his face. But his dander was up: the burning contempt made him feel a whole lot better. It also served to sharpen his wits. He gave a mocking laugh of derision. Tocahatchi's scowling response indicated that he understood only too well the gist of the ridicule.

'Whatever would the great Shongopovi think if'n he knew the kind of lowlife son he had spawned?'

A howl of rage issued from the Indian's gaping mouth as he lunged forward. Bat repelled the surging thrust. Steel blades clashed, ringing loud in the still air. Backing off the two men circled warily, each eyeing the other's body language, waiting for an opportunity to attack.

Back and forth they fought, lunging and parrying as the lethal contest was played out to its bitter finale.

Tocahatchi tried scooping up a handful of sand and throwing it into his opponent's face. But Bearclaw had learned from his previous encounter and turned his head away, greeting the feeble tactic with a harsh guffaw.

'You're gonna have to do a sight better'n that, redman.'

Tocahatchi growled at the taunt like an enraged bear.

And so it went on.

Fifteen minutes passed. Bat was losing ever more blood from the gash in his left arm. The wound was throbbing. His concentration was beginning to flag. Much more of this and he would be at the bastard's mercy, and it was a certainty that none of *that* would be shown.

Then disaster struck.

Bat tripped over a rock and fell on to his back. With a howl of jubilation the Indian saw his chance.

'Now white dog pay for his insults.' So the varmint had understood, after all. There was no time for any other random thoughts. Already the killer was pitching in for the denouement.

But help was at hand from an unlikely source.

The paint must have sensed in her befuggled state that her master was in dire straits. With one last supreme effort, the mare stumbled on to shaky legs and surged at the Indian from one side. The lowered head struck Tocahatchi in the shoulder, knocking him to the ground.

Certain death had suddenly been averted. Bat took full advantage of this unexpected lifeline. His hand brushed the necklace of claws in thanksgiving. But there was no further time for speculation.

Grabbing up the fallen knife he dived on to the sprawling Indian before the brave could comprehend his opponent's unexpected reprieve. He pressed a knee hard into his adversary's back, pinning the critter to the ground. He raised the deadly knife blade ready for the *coup de grâce*.

It descended, but stopped an inch from the exposed back.

This was not Bat Madison's way. The Navajo was at his mercy, and of that Bat would allow no doubt. But there was one other way that he could achieve a victory far more poignant than death could ever be for a proud Navajo.

Reversing the knife he slammed down the hilt on to the exposed head. Tocahatchi grunted. He was not out cold, but was sufficiently stupefied to enable Bat to carry out his grim task undisturbed.

'Killing you would be too easy,' the white man snarled triumphantly.

With a single yank, he tore off the Indian's headband, releasing the flowing black locks. One hand gripped the thick mass of hair while the other sawed at the roots close to the victim's scalp.

Jumping to his feet, Bat threw the howling Indian on to his back. He jammed a hefty boot on to the red man's heaving chest. The white man couldn't restrain a malevolent leer as he gazed down at the distraught Indian, shaking the dirty hank in the brave's face.

The final insult was to throw the hair down and grind it into the dust with his boot heel.

Tocahatchi bayed like a wounded beast. The macabre wail sounded as if his very heart had been ripped from his breast. Bat could almost feel sorry for the Indian. But it was only a fleeting sentiment. The critter deserved to suffer.

'This is a far more appropriate punishment for the likes of you.' He glared down at his defeated foe. The knife was held ready to finish the job should Tocahatchi show any resistance. Then he moved back a pace growling. 'Now get up and shift your damned ass.'

The knife was quickly sheathed and replaced by a notched bow and arrow.

The Indian was speechless with woe.

He had lost all motivation to fight. In truth, the removal of his hair had sapped his strength. All the glory and status he had earned as an august Navajo brave now counted for nought. Had the Indian known, his situation was akin to that depicted in the biblical story of Samson and Delilah. Bat smiled at the connection. It made for a fitting comparison.

Cowed and beaten, Tocahatchi picked up his fallen knife and slunk away into the arid wasteland: a lowly creature reduced to something no better than the other wild scavengers of the desert.

But the conflict had not gone all Bat Madison's way. His horse now lay on the ground gasping out its final seconds of life. Saving her master had been the straw that broke the camel's back. And Bat's injury was worse than he had feared. He moved across to the Indian's pony.

All Indians carried a medicine bag. The one fastened to the bridle was larger than usual on account of Tocahatchi's supposed task at Medicine Gap. Many of the tribal remedies had been passed down through generations of shamans and were highly effective cures for all manner of afflictions.

Bat delved inside. He soon found what he was seeking.

Yarrow was a plant effective for preventing the spread of infection from cuts and bruises. It also helped to clot the blood and thus encouraged the wound to heal much faster. After applying the salve to the raw gash, he bandaged it up with cloth from a spare shirt.

As for the horse, he could do little to ease its suffering. Without a gun to quicken the inevitable, the animal would be at the mercy of wandering bands of coyotes. Bat was not prepared to allow that to happen. So he stayed with the loyal beast, stroking its noble head and murmuring endearments into its ear.

The end was not long in coming.

Tears etched a trail down the the white man's dust-caked visage. The paint had served him well over the years. They had ridden many trails, shared a host of adventures together. Unlike many frontiersmen who treated their mounts as nothing more than useful tools, the pair had forged a strong bond of companionship.

With a heavy heart he rose to his feet and set about removing his saddle. He slung it across the back of the Indian's mustang. Luckily the cayuse was well broken and offered no objections to this strange accoutrement.

THIRTEEN

FATAL CHOICE

Bat did not linger in the vicinity of the brutal ambush.

Urging the mustang forward on this last leg of his journey to Medicine Gap, he thoroughly scanned the surrounding prospect for signs of the humiliated Indian. But Tocahatchi had disappeared, swallowed up by the terrain he was now condemned to inhabit.

It was some time before Bat was able to push the cayuse to more than a gentle plod. His arm still throbbed, although the searing pain had faded. An hour passed, after which he nudged the horse up to a steady canter. The miles were soon eaten up and he began to feel more like his old self.

But the mood of despondency took some time to lift.

His spirits were cheered a little by the playful antics of some prairie dogs playing chase between the stands of yucca. The game brought a smile to the rider's grim features.

But where there is light, the darkness soon follows. A hawk dropped like a stone from the cloudless sky. There followed a squeal of terror as the bird rose into the shimmering sky clutching its prey.

Survival of the fittest. As in the animal kingdom, so it was with humans. Bat still had to reach Medicine Gap and complete his duty of escorting the lovely Eleanor Newbold to Albuquerque.

Then there was the problem of Pike Roswell to consider. The varmint was not going to give up the chance of earning twenty grand without a fight. How and when he would make his move was in the lap of the gods. All Bat could do was keep his wits sharp and his eyes open.

The cunning outlaw was at that moment hunched over a mug of coffee beside a campfire. He glanced across at the woman who was scouring the pans with sand. Over on the far side of the clearing Frank was checking the cayuses' nosebags. No difficulties had been experienced in finding Medicine Gap.

The great rent in the rock wall was a half-mile in width. It was filled with boulders and shattered rocks fallen from the weakened fault line. The gap itself was a mile deep and could be seen well before it was reached. On the far side more of the same broken rock and sandy terrain stretched away into the distance.

Roswell sucked on a cheroot staring into the campfire. Dancing tendrils of flame were reflected in his black eyes. The outlaw's devious brain was busily working out a plan of action. Various options had been assessed and discarded.

Seeds of doubt had already been planted in the woman's mind regarding her paladin's trustworthiness. Frank's wavering attitude appeared to have been squashed.

All that Pike Roswell needed to do now was to remove the thorn in his side. That was the reason he had chosen their current campsite behind a cluster of rocks. It was hidden from view and afforded an ideal spot from which to set an ambush.

Roswell flipped open the lid of his gold watch. He gave a satisfied nod. Time was on his side. He estimated that Madison ought to be appearing around late afternoon. By then the sun would have sunk below the high bluffs to the west. No chance for the course of action upon which he had resolved being impeded.

He stood up, flicked the cigar butt into the fire.

'Over here, Frank,' he called across to his partner while moving away from the woman. What he had to say was between the two of them.

Craddock laid aside his own mount's nosebag and sauntered over to join Roswell. 'What's on your mind, Pike?' he asked innocently.

'I want you up on that bluff.' He pointed to a stack of slabbed rocks that gave the appearance of a kid's abandoned set of building blocks. 'From up there you'll have an uninterrupted view west to give me warning of Madison's arrival.'

Frank's body tensed. Lines of puzzlement ribbed

his brow. 'What's that supposed to mean?' he said stiffly. 'Why do you need any warning?'

Roswell picked up on his partner's hesitation. 'Didn't we agree that Madison needs to be eliminated?' He then proceeded to answer his own question. 'And there's only one sure way to do that. Kill the jasper before he kills us.'

'Bat wouldn't do that,' Frank objected. 'He ain't that kinda guy.' The younger man's shoulders lifted. His eyes narrowed, his thick eyebrows meeting in a suspicious frown. His whole body was a reaction against the notion of staging a bushwhacking. 'And neither am I. Figured you knew that.'

'Don't be such a greenhorn,' Roswell sneered. 'You have to take what life hands out, any which way you are able. And if'n that means using foul means, so what? That's the name of the game.' The gang leader's sap was rising. At this stage in his plans there was no place for any shilly-shallying.

'You joined up with me knowing the score. We've robbed stagecoaches, broken into stores and fleeced those carrying too much dough for their own good. Men have been killed. This is no different. There ain't no going back now. Both of us are in this for keeps.'

'You knew that me and Tom didn't hold with back-shooters and lowlife bushwhackers when you asked us to join you. Sure we've killed, but it was face to face.'

Roswell was seething. The jibe rankled. But like all men who live by their wits, he held his temper firmly in check. Lose your rag and you lose the fight was a good axiom to live by. He should have known that a chucklehead like Frank Craddock always lived by his own jaundiced code of fair play.

The writing was now on the wall.

'So what are you saying, Frank?' The demand for clarification fizzed out like a cork from a bottle.

'I don't want no part of this so I'm pulling out.' Turning his back on Roswell, Frank Craddock walked purposefully towards where his horse was idly nudging the fallen nosebag.

'No you ain't,' hissed Roswell. 'Nobody quits my gang until I say so.'

The threat was ignored as Craddock swung up into the saddle.

Black malevolent eyes skewered the younger man. 'Does this mean that you're gonna warn Madison?'

'He can fight his own battles,' Craddock shot back while walking his horse to the edge of the clearing. 'But I want no part of it.'

Roswell didn't believe him. Soon as he was out of sight the varmint would swing west to join up with his old partner.

'You have one more chance to see sense,' shouted Roswell at the retreating back as he moved across to his own horse. Silently he withdrew the Winchester from its scabbard. 'Join me now and we can both be rich men.'

'*Adios amigo,*' came the distant response.

Roswell's thin lips stretched wide in an angry grimace. Purposely, loudly, he jacked a fresh round into the chamber of his rifle.

A buzzard cawed high on the bluff. Wings fluttered

with excitement as the bird sensed that the climax to the grim scenario was about to be played out.

Closely observing the showdown of which she was a major cast member, Eleanor Newbold held her breath. The dirty pots and pans were abandoned. She wanted to shout a warning to the other man. But the shock of witnessing cold-blooded murder about to take place had frozen her reactions.

'You had your chance, kid,' the killer whispered to himself as he made to pull the trigger. 'This is what happens to skunks that wear a Judas coat.'

Just in time he slackened his finger.

Madison could have made better time than expected. Firing the rifle might well alert the critter that skulduggery was afoot. The sound of gunfire carried long distances in the dry air of the desert. Quickly he drew a knife from its leather boot sheath. In a single reflex action, it was sent winging through the static air.

The missile was right on target.

Craddock threw up his arms as the lethal blade punched him hard in the back. Simultaneously, a scream of terror erupted from the woman's mouth. It came too late. Frank slewed sideways out of the saddle. But his boot caught in the stirrup. The panic-stricken cayuse bolted off, dragging its rider along the rough ground.

Eleanor stared agog at the disappearing cayuse and its gruesome load. For seconds only, she remained rooted to the spot, unable to move or utter another sound. Then her gaze swung towards the cold-blooded perpetrator of the foul deed. Her mouth opened wide. A scream of fear and revulsion emerged in a long-drawn-out wail.

Roswell hurried across and grabbed the woman, planting a hand of death across her mouth. A shrieking dame was infinitely worse than gunfire. Hot lead could mean anything. But here in Medicine Gap a panicking woman meant only one thing. Madison would instinctively know that Eleanor Newbold was in trouble.

The hand tightened across her mouth, the other encircled her body in a vicelike grip. Then a gruff voice penetrated the woman's addled brain.

'I'm going to remove my hand,' the macabre crackle hissed in her ear. 'Another outburst like that and I'll wrap a gag around that pretty mouth of your'n. Understand me, sister?'

The woman's eyes bulged alarmingly as her head bobbed.

The stifling hand gingerly eased off, allowing her to breathe deeply. Having regained her composure, Eleanor eyed the killer with undisguised loathing.

'So this was your plan all along, was it?' she spat out accusingly. 'Kill off your partners and ambush Bat. That way the whole reward for my return would be yours.'

A leery smirk cracked the lined face. 'You got the drift, lady. Clever, eh? Pike Roswell ain't such a no-account desperado after all. Hand you in and collect the dough. Then I can disappear and have me a high old time down Mexico way, where the whiskey's cheap and the gals are even cheaper.' He bellowed uproariously at his witticism.

'If you think that I won't spill the beans on your sickening actions, then you must be mad,' the woman rapped back. 'You'll be arrested and I'll be at the trial to give evidence and see you hang for your despicable crimes.'

Her elegant nose twitched imperiously as she regarded the outlaw like a piece of dirt.

Roswell snarled. His rough hand grabbed the woman by her arm and shook her. 'Think I'm some kinda greenhorn?' he growled. Flint-hard eyes bored deep into the woman's very soul. 'You ain't gonna say a blamed word against me. And I'll tell you why.'

The tight grip relaxed. A sly look replaced the dark scowl of moments earlier. Before revealing his *pièce de résistance*, the braggart extracted a cigar and lit up. He inhaled, enjoying the taste of the fine Havana.

'When I've finished revealing all that took place in that Indian camp, your fine upstanding fiancé will want nothing more to do with you.'

'Nothing happened that I'm ashamed of,' the woman protested. 'Shongopovi treated me fairly. Life was tough but he never laid a finger on me.'

Roswell hawked out a brutal guffaw. 'Think old Howard is gonna believe that? Why else were you taken if not to satisfy that savage's animal lust? After all, ain't that what Indians are, savages that live off the land just like the creatures of the desert?'

'Howard loves me, he would never believe a killer

like you over the word of his fiancée.'

'The guy is a wealthy and highly respected landowner who don't want anything to upset his standing in the community. Anything that smells of scandal and he'll run a mile.' Roswell thrust his chin at the girl. 'I've seen him, lady. Strutting his stuff up and down Albuquerque's main drag and lapping up all the bowing and scraping from lesser men.'

'He wouldn't abandon me, he wouldn't,' the woman exclaimed. 'Why should he believe a skunk like you over his beloved wife?'

'Because he's a man going places,' Roswell punched out. 'Rumour has it that Howard Thompson aims to run for territorial governor at the next election. Think he wants to be saddled with a tainted wife for such an important job? Even if'n he does harbour suspicions that I'm making it all up, mud sticks. And my reckoning is that he won't want to take that risk.'

'You're wrong! You're wrong! We love each other, that's all that matters.' But was it? Tears were trickling down her cheeks. It was true that Howard was a very ambitious man. Yet still she persisted in denying what was staring her in the face. 'I just do not believe he would act that way.'

However, there was more than a hint of desperation in the refusal to believe in such a cold reaction from her fiancé.

The plaintive utterance brought a smirk of triumph to the killer's leering visage. He knew that seeds of doubt were sprouting fast. Eleanor had tried to inject a tone of vigorous denial into her voice. But it lacked any conviction.

Roswell now moved in for the kill.

'And believe me, lady. Pike Roswell can be very persuasive when his life is at stake. Once I've finished spouting off, he'll believe everything I've told him. Take it from me, there ain't gonna be no wedding.'

The killer waited for the force of his argument to sink in. The stupefied expression on Eleanor's pale features told him all he wanted to know.

'So,' Roswell snapped out. 'Is it a deal? You gonna play ball, lady, and keep quiet? Then you can continue to enjoy the good life, while old Pike here gets to do the same for returning you safe and sound to the loving arms of a doting fiancé.'

Eleanor just sat there, unable to comprehend the bizarre turn of events.

Roswell uttered a growl of irritation. 'Make up your mind, gal. I ain't got all day.'

The prodding blade of the knife helped speed up her response. A slow nod was all that Roswell needed. His tight jaws relaxed, a sigh of relief issued from between gritted teeth. His fist clenched in jubilation as he scuttled over to his horse.

He unfurled the lariat and wasted no time in securing the woman's arms and legs. Before she could recover her senses, a grubby bandanna had been tied across her mouth. The last thing the schemer needed now was for a warning shout to alert the approaching Bearclaw Bat Madison.

FOURTEEN

A GHOSTLY SHOWDOWN

Bat had made much better time than expected.

A sandstorm had blown up, forcing him to hunker down behind his horse. The wind had screeched and buffeted both man and beast, driving them into the ground like a tent-peg. An unremitting blast of sand had vehemently striven to dislodge this impediment from its path. The continuous howl was deafening. When would it end? Such storms could last for days.

Fortunately the storm had been moving from north to south across his route. It passed over within the hour. The keening sound faded, the wind died, and the sun returned, a welcome orb in the clear sky.

Crawling out from beneath a blanket of gritty sand, Bat shook himself like a dog. A cloud of soft

ochre drifted in the light breeze. The mustang likewise lumbered to its feet. It took a further half-hour
to get rid of the grainy mantle that had smothered
everything.

Back on the trail Bat pushed the horse to a surging
gallop, anxious to make up for lost time.

It was mid-afternoon when the familiar rock for-
mations of Medicine Gap hove into view. The
approach was across a featureless plain which rose
gradually to meet the huge split in the rock wall.

A roadrunner suddenly veered in from the right.
This strange relation of the cuckoo could achieve a
remarkable turn of speed as it loped with ungainly
haste on its long spindly legs. When it caught sight of
the human interloper, the bird scooted away, to disappear in a clump of ocatillo. Bat couldn't help but
smile at the amusing spectacle.

But then something alarming caught his eye: a
plume of dust.

It was moving at a rapid pace even though the air
was still. All too soon it resolved into the shape of a
riderless horse.

Bat whipped out his telescope and sighted it on to
the mysterious phenomenon. His assumption was
that the animal must have come from those camped
in Medicine Gap. So what had happened there to
cause a horse to flee?

Adjusting the focus of the spyglass, Bat followed the
progress of the approaching animal. Then his mouth
dropped open. A man was being dragged along the
ground, his left boot stuck fast in the stirrup.

Bat drew his own mount to a halt and waited for the galloping cayuse to draw near. Unhooking the lariat, he shook it loose to form a large loop. He then wrapped half its length around his saddle horn. As the other horse drew level he spurred his own mount to go parallel and tossed the loop over the animal's bobbing head.

The rope tightened. At the same time Bat dragged hard on his reins, urging the mustang to dig its hoofs into the sand. The tough little Indian pony skidded to a juddering halt. Smoke rose from the friction burn as the rope buzzed around the horn.

Bat's action succeeded in slowing down the panic-stricken horse with its gruesome cargo. The animal snorted, its hoofs pawing the ground. Its steaming flanks were wreathed in lather.

Bat leapt from his mount and hurried across to identify the fallen rider.

Blood drained from his tanned features as he stared down at the dead man. Frank Craddock was barely recognizable, so severe had been the battering to which his now lacerated body had been subjected.

For a long minute Bat stood mesmerized by the bleeding torso that had once been a human being. Then his searching gaze fastened on to the knife that was still stuck fast into the dead man's back. A seething rage gripped his innards. This had to be the work of Pike Roswell.

Lines of hate ribbed his brow.

So the double-dealing skunk had already set his

plans in motion. Clearly, Roswell and Frank Craddock must have had a serious disagreement. They had argued. Frank had made to leave and Roswell had killed him. What the backstabber had not counted on was Frank's horse taking flight.

Now the crazy bastard would be up there, ready and waiting.

Once again Bat put the glass to his eye. Panning the distant terrain, he searched for a clue to the presence of his treacherous ex-partner. Then he saw it: a thin wisp of smoke rising above some bluffs.

At least now he had some proper weapons and a saddle horse with which to challenge and defeat his enemy.

'You ain't died in vain, Frank,' he murmured while hauling the gruesome remains behind a cluster of rocks. 'And I'll make darned sure you are avenged for what that lowlife has done.'

Having no spade, he jabbed at the hard ground with his knife. It took a half-hour to dig a shallow grave into which he laid the corpse. Stones were placed over the top to prevent any desecration from scavenging coyotes. Satisfied that he had shown due respect for the dead man, Bat removed his hat to mutter a few words of condolence over the makeshift grave.

Labouring over the grim duty had given him time to figure out how best to get the drop on Pike Roswell without endangering the woman's safety. Even though the reward on Eleanor Newbold was substantial, Roswell would not think twice about holding her life to ransom should his own worthless hide be threatened.

He removed the saddle and tack from the Indian pony and slapped the animal on its hind quarters.

'Off you go, fella,' he grunted. 'Back to where you came from.' The horse whinnied a reply before galloping off.

Slowly Bat mounted the saddle horse. He extracted Frank's Henry carbine and checked that the magazine had a full load. He also checked the Schofield, which was double-action and a heavier gun than he was used to. He hefted the revolver in his right hand, getting used to its feel.

With the rifle resting on his thighs, Bat nudged the horse towards the distant Gap. Ominous thoughts flicked through his mind. Was Roswell even now watching his old buddy from cover, just itching for him to come within range?

The thought pulled the Texan up in his tracks.

He vividly recalled how Pike Roswell had earned a reputation for stealth and cunning during the war. A shady operator who could sneak into the enemy's camp, destroy an ammunition dump, then disappear like a bad dream. Was it any wonder that the Union had labelled him *The Ghost?*

Bat swung wide of the main entrance to Medicine Gap and tethered his horse behind some rocks. In such broken terrain, he felt that the rifle would hinder his movements. A pistol was the best option.

Bent low, he scuttled between the various outcrops, eyes constantly searching for any alien presence. Nerves were strung tight as a drawn bow string. Bearclaw Madison would have much preferred to face a rampant grizzly than this crafty opponent known as *The Ghost*.

Slowly and carefully he gained height, edging his way towards the rising tendrils of smoke. As he crossed the entrance to a narrow gully a shot rang out. Fragments of rock showered the hunched stalker. Out of the corner of his eye he saw a shadow looming at the top end of the gully. But it had vanished when he swung round to face it.

A harsh laugh cut through the tense atmosphere.

'Could have had you there, old buddy. You're gonna have to do a sight better if'n you want to catch the Ghost.'

The brittle challenge sent a cold shiver down Bat's spine. He felt like a fish being baited. With his back flat against the rock wall, he listened intently. But there was no further sound. The Ghost had disappeared into the rocky crevasse.

Bat circled around the base of the cliff, drawing ever closer to where he judged Roswell's camp to be situated. Every step was calculated to prevent the deadly apparition from anticipating his next move. He could only pray that he had the measure of the lethal fisherman.

Then he saw it.

Crouched at the edge of the clearing, he had an open view of the camp. And there, on the far side, was Eleanor Newbold. She was securely gagged and tethered. But of Roswell there was no sign. So what

149

should he do? Reveal himself? That would be playing into the hands of the merciless skunk. The alternative of remaining hidden, however, was an equally risky option.

A decision had to made.

Exercising due caution, he crept around the outer rim of the clearing. Eventually he reached a position just behind where the woman was lying. This was going to be his best chance of freeing her. By reaching around the side of the boulder against which she was leaning he would have just enough room to slice through her bonds with his knife without revealing his presence.

'Pssst!' he hissed through clenched teeth. 'Miss Newbold. Eleanor. It's me, Bat Madison.'

The woman's body stiffened, indicating that she had heard him. Her head turned, terrified red-rimmed eyes met those of her rescuer.

'Just edge your body to this side so's I can reach your hands,' he whispered 'I don't want to show myself in case Roswell is near by.'

Anxiously Bat's gaze searched the immediate terrain. Nothing moved. His white knuckles gripped the knife handle as he reached out and began sawing at the tight ropes.

Within a few minutes they parted. Eleanor rubbed her stiff and sore wrists, then tore the filthy gag from her mouth.

'Thank goodness you came,' she blurted out, tears welling up as the emotion of being rescued once again threatened to overwhelm her. 'Roswell killed

Craddock because Frank wanted no part of ambushing you. Then he threatened to tell all kinds of lies to Howard if I didn't go along with his odious scheme to claim the reward.'

She burst into tears.

Her rescuer knew that this was not the time for protracted explanations. Roswell could not be far away. The sooner they disappeared, the better.

'Come on,' he pressed, helping her up. 'We have to get out of here fast before Roswell turns up.'

'Too late for that, old buddy.' The casual announcement, although half-expected, came as a stunning jolt. Roswell coughed out a brittle laugh. Then in a more brusque tone he rapped, 'Now shuck that pistol and get your hands up.'

Bat felt his skin crawling. Seconds earlier he had assiduously checked around to ensure there was no sign of Roswell. Yet here he was. The Ghost had lost none of his shadowy skills during the intervening years.

Slowly Bat turned around to face the elusive wraith. His gun fell to the ground as his hands lifted.

'Surely you didn't figure to outwit a professional assassin, did you, old buddy?' The leering query needed no answer and was accompanied by another hearty guffaw. 'Still,' Roswell conceded with a mock-magnanimous gesture, 'you almost had me fooled when you doubled back from that gully.'

Roswell snap-levered the Winchester. It was a deliberate action intended to leave Bat in no doubt regarding the outcome of their brief *tête-a-tête*. The killer saw his adversary's muscles stiffen.

'Don't try anything stupid,' he rasped. 'I'm taking the girl on to Albuquerque alone.' He paused as if contemplating an important decision. 'Trouble is, if'n I spare you, I'll be having to look over my shoulder for evermore.' He shook his head. 'Can't be doing with that.'

The Winchester rose.

FIFTEEN

REPRIEVE

A shot echoed round the clearing.

Roswell staggered back clutching at his shoulder. His face registered total surprise. Desperately, he tried to raise the rifle. Two more bullets punched him in the chest. He sank to his knees, blood pouring from his wounds. The gun slipped from nerveless fingers as he toppled over; a dark patch spread beneath the riddled corpse.

For what seemed like a lifetime, Bat stood rooted to the spot, unable to comprehend the reprieve from certain death. Slowly he peered about him, wondering who could have come to his aid. A rider emerged from behind a high pinnacle of rock. Slowly he picked a course between the chaotic jumble of rocks. The butt of a Winchester rested on his bronzed thigh. Sticking out from his headband were three eagle feathers; a string of luck beads jogged around

153

the patrician neck.

It was Shongopovi.

The Indian chief drew to a halt beside the dead body.

All that Madison could offer was a brief nod of acknowledgement followed by the simple query: 'What is the great chief, Shongopovi, doing here at Medicine Gap?' He was still in shock. Snatched from the jaws of death yet again.

'You have Little White Dove to thank. She it was who did not trust her brother when he pressed to accompany you here,' the chief declared, remaining on his horse. 'I was persuaded by her words of wisdom. So I followed and found the outcast wandering in desert. A goatskin of water persuaded him to tell truth. Once again you spared his life after being ambushed. But he will not be welcomed back into tribe this time.'

Eleanor was clinging on to Bat's arm. Her whole body was trembling from the aftermath of the ordeal.

Listening to what Shongopovi had to say gave Bat time to recover from his near-death experience.

Such calls were becoming a habit he could well do without.

The first time had been back at the Bitter Creek trading post, when Roswell had saved him; then his horse had butted in when Tocahatchi was all set to deliver the final verdict. Now it was Shongopovi's turn to join the sequence.

Bat was beginning to think that he was living on borrowed time. He shook off the macabre thought.

'We are grateful for your intervention, great chief of the Navajo,' he intoned. 'Now I will be able to complete my mission to conduct this lady back to her worried fiancé in Albuquerque.'

'It is I who have much to thank you for, white man,' said the Indian. 'The life of my daughter means much to me. And perhaps some day my dishonourable son will be able to appease the great spirit.' He swung the horse around to leave. 'And now I go to seek out the herbs and plants so important for my people.'

With that he laid the Winchester on a nearby slab of rock and departed.

Bat smiled. The old guy wasn't such a bad cuss after all.

It was too late in the day to leave; the pair were forced to remain at the grisly scene for the night. Bat covered the body of Pike Roswell with the guy's own saddle blanket.

Then he suddenly remembered that he hadn't eaten since the previous day.

'I'm ravenous,' he informed the woman. 'Any chance of you rustling up some vittles while I go find my horse?'

For the first time in a coon's age Eleanor's face cracked into a wide grin. The change was amazing. From a morose and downcast fugitive she was instantly transformed into the beautiful princess of storybooks.

Bat's heart skipped a beat. For once he was struck dumb. Embarrassment was evident on his ruddy cheeks. He turned away while the woman set about collecting some kindling.

There was only one cloud hanging over her new-found joy. But for the moment she kept that to herself.

They set off early the next morning. Albuquerque was only a day's ride. By maintaining a brisk pace, Bat estimated they could be there around sundown.

For the first hour a strange silence lay between them. The rather tense atmosphere of the past night seemed to remain. Eleanor was betrothed to another. Bat had his duty to continue the search for his lost wife.

Then as they rode, the woman plucked up the courage to raise the matter that had been troubling her for some time. It was none other than the despicable Pike Roswell who had brought it tumbling to the forefront of her thoughts.

It was true that Howard was a very ambitious man. Prestige and status in the eyes of those in authority had always been a priority for him. Business before pleasure.

Could it be that he really would have dropped her like a hot brick once the notion suggested by Roswell had been planted in his mind? Why had he not come looking for her instead of merely getting others to do the onerous work for a price? Was he swayed by love, or the need for a well-bred woman on his arm? After all she was the daughter of an important congress-man.

These and other doubts now posed an alarming quandary. The dark cloud of her bleak musing blotted out the warmth of the rising sun. Bat picked up on the woman's aura of melancholy.

'Something troubling you, Eleanor?' he asked as they jogged along side by side. 'You seem a tad cool. And the sun's well up now.' He tried to make light of the woman's obvious remoteness.

For a moment she was silent, considering how to voice her uncertainty.

'Do you ever have . . . doubts that your wife might never be found?' she asked hesitantly.

Now it was Bat's turn to assume a solemn expression.

It was a question he had often considered but had kept hidden deep within his subconscious. Now, like a simmering volcano, it had been prodded back to life with a vengeance.

It was Eleanor Newbold who had resurrected the unwelcome thought.

Her tight, rather pinched look said it all. The woman reached out a hand. Her touch sent a rippling tingle through his body. He gripped her hand. Turning to face her, he felt himself drowning in those deep mesmerizing orbs. The truth was out, and both of them knew it, though it was Eleanor who made the tentative suggestion.

'Do you think that we might possibly have a future together?' The fiery pools of light willed this tall handsome paladin to concur.

But he did not get the chance to reply.

A rattle of sliding stones broke on to his dreamy deliberations. Instantly his mind switched back into hunter mode. A shadow appeared on the trail ahead. Its origin was on the ledge under which they were about to pass. Some alien presence up there had inadvertantly dislodged the loose stones.

Out the corner of his eye he saw it: a blurred form flying through the air like a striking eagle. In the creature's paw glinted a knife raised to strike death and destruction to this, its sworn enemy. The face of Tocahatchi, snarling and twisted with hate, loomed into view.

Eleanor screamed.

In a single smooth action, Bat slapped leather and palmed the preferred Colt Frontier that he had reclaimed. Three shots blasted forth. The Indian continued his headlong dive, forcing Bat to swing his horse aside. The dead body of the Indian crashed to the ground.

Bat calmly peered down at the bleeding corpse. Then he realized how the disgraceful Indian had managed to overtake them. The released mustang must have somehow been drawn by its master's odour. Unfortunately for Tocahatchi, over-eagerness to seek revenge had made him careless.

Bat fingered the magic talisman encircling his neck.

'It sure wasn't your lucky day when you met up with Bat Madison,' he murmured, blowing the smoke off the barrel of the revolver. He slipped the gun back into its holster. He shook his head in mock admonishment of the lifeless Indian. 'Some jiggers just ain't got no manners.'

Then he turned back to face the horror-struck woman.

'Now what was that you were saying afore this critter muscled in on our private conflab? Something about us joining up.'

Violence once again had reached out its icy hand in the Socorro desert of New Mexico. But Eleanor Newbold couldn't help but feel secure under this unique man's ardent gaze. Her countenance exuded a radiant vivacity.

The future suddenly appeared to be much more enticing.